Year 4

CW00868303

Tilly Millpepper

and the

Wishing Stone

Tilly Millpepper

and the

Wishing Stone

J.E. NARRACOTT

CAVALCADE BOOKS

First published in the United Kingdom in 2019

by Cavalcade Books
www.cavalcadebooks.com

Copyright © J.E. Narracott 2019

The moral right of the author has been asserted.
All rights reserved.

No part of this publication may be reproduced, stored in a
retrieval system, or transmitted, in any form or by any means,
without the prior permission in writing of the publisher, nor be
otherwise circulated in any form of binding or cover other than
that in which it is published and without a similar condition
including this condition being imposed on the subsequent
purchaser.

ISBN 978-1-9996213-6-0

This is a work of fiction. The story, all names, characters and
incidents portrayed in this book are fictitious. No identification
with actual persons (living or deceased), places, buildings and
products is intended or should be inferred.

Illustrations and cover design by Nina Taylor
www.taylormaiddesigns.co.uk

For Sam, my handsome horsey friend,
who came into my life during my teens
just when I needed him.
Thank you, Sam.
I will never forget you.

.

Contents

CHAPTER 1

The Birthday Girl

THIS IS the extraordinary tale of Tilly Millpepper who lived with her parents and her teenage brother, Bradley, at number 18, Park Street, North London. The Millpeppers had lived in this small terraced Victorian house, with its ivy-covered walls, ever since Wendy and Archie (now known as Mum and Dad) were married some fifteen years ago. They had bought the house because it was near to where Archie's parents lived. In fact, it was *very* near – right next door. Archie's parents (known as Grammy and Poppa) lived at number 16.

Every weekday morning at six o'clock precisely, Dad – a tall, lean man with curly, auburn hair and steel rimmed glasses – rose from his bed and prepared himself for the day ahead. Then, as the grandfather clock in the hall struck seven-thirty, with his tie suitably knotted, he would kiss his wife and children goodbye and head for the front door. Once out in the street, he would turn left and walk quickly towards the bus stop at the corner. A red London double-decker bus would take him to his office job where he would sit behind a computer all day, tapping at the keys and answering the phone.

Mum didn't start work until later in the day, so she made sure the children arrived at school for eight-thirty each morning. Her job was more interesting than her husband's. She was a chef. But she too had to work long hours. There was a set routine for the whole family, week in week out, and it was all a bit boring. However, that was about to change, and it all started with Tilly's tenth birthday.

It was a Monday morning in early June and for once the sun was out. Hearing a familiar sound, freckled-faced Tilly opened her sleepy hazel eyes and was immediately aware of a furry face staring back at her. Jellicle, her black and white cat, was sitting on top of her purring loudly. This wasn't an unusual occurrence because Jellicle truly believed it was as much her bed as it was Tilly's.

"Morning Jelly, do you know what today is?" asked Tilly, reaching out and stroking her cat's head. Enjoying the attention, Jellicle placed a white-socked paw on Tilly's cheek and began to purr even louder. "Of course you do, because you're the cleverest and most beautiful cat in the whole world. Today," Tilly continued, "is my birthday! Do you think Mum will say I don't have to go to school?"

"Sorry, nice try, but even birthday girls have to go to school," laughed Mum as she entered Tilly's bedroom. She was quite a short woman – much shorter than her husband – and her brown hair was cut in a bob, resting just above her shoulders. "Happy birthday, Tilly!" Bending over her daughter she gave her a kiss on the cheek. "Now up you get. Dad and Bradley are waiting downstairs to give you your presents."

And there they were, her dad and her brother, waiting patiently for the birthday girl. Actually, that wasn't completely true. Dad was engrossed in a craft magazine and Bradley was playing a game on his iPhone. Nevertheless, they both lifted their heads to wish Tilly a happy birthday and Dad gave her a big kiss and a hug.

Seeing the kitchen table covered in brightly wrapped parcels, Tilly squealed with delight. She opened each of her gifts – clothes, books and vouchers – with a polite smile. However, the best present of all was a highly-decorated skateboard. She couldn't wait to try it out later at the skatepark across the street.

"Here, Short Stuff," said Bradley, throwing a crudely-wrapped parcel in Tilly's direction. "I hope you like it." Returning his gaze to his iPhone he added, "Don't blame me if you don't. It was

Mum who said you would."

Thirteen-year-old Bradley, whose recently cut dark hair was short on the sides with a quiff on the top, was at that certain age when everything other than his friends or computers was 'boring' or 'too much trouble'. Certainly, his younger sister came under the category of 'too much trouble'.

Tilly tore uneasily at the paper, remembering the present Bradley had brought her last year – a pair of pink socks – knowing full well that, unlike most of her friends, Tilly hated the colour pink. This gift, though, delighted her. It was a multi-coloured woollen hat with earflaps.

"Thanks, Bradders. I love my blue one like this. I've been wanting it in another colour for ages."

"You're welcome," he managed to reply, whilst still concentrating on his game.

"Come on, everyone, we'd better get moving!" cried Mum as she began to clear the table. "Archie, look at the clock. You'll be late! Bradley, are you ready for school? I don't want you rushing around at the last minute looking for your PE bag. Go on, get yourself sorted."

Mumbling to himself in a frequency only other teenagers can understand, Bradley's shoulders dropped as he stomped his way to the bathroom.

Reluctantly stepping off her skateboard, Tilly tore back upstairs, threw on her school uniform and dragged a brush through her thick, curly, auburn hair before pulling it back into a ponytail. There, she at least was ready for the day ahead.

CHAPTER 2

Uncle Leonardo

TILLY AND her mum arrived at school just in time to hear the registration bell. Kissing Mum at the gate, Tilly ran to join her friends and together they made their way through the main door of the school.

In the classroom she sat next to her best friend Leila, whose black hair was braided into two neat plaits. They listened quietly to their teacher, Mrs Brown, as she read out the names on the register.

Tilly and Leila had been friends since infants and they spent a lot of time together in and out of school. Leila's dad, Lloyd, was from Jamaica and as a consequence her family would often holiday on the Caribbean Island. Tilly loved hearing Leila's tales about her family out there, so much so, she dreamed about visiting Jamaica herself one day.

Resting her chin in her hands with her elbows on her desk, Tilly smiled to herself. Mrs Brown was a very petite woman with the tiniest of eyes. One day in the playground Tilly had referred to her as Mrs Mouse, making her friends laugh. Now the name had stuck and everyone called her Mrs Mouse – not to her face, of course. They wouldn't dare.

"I see," Mrs Brown began, "that two of you have birthdays today. Tilly and Shaun, would you both join me at the front of the class, please?"

Reluctantly, Tilly got to her feet. Every year since she'd started school, she'd had to share her 'special day' with Shaun: an irritating boy who was always picking his nose. It was so embarrassing. Standing facing her classmates, Tilly's face blushed as the whole class began to sing, "*Happy Birthday to you* …" It was the same ritual for everyone when it was their birthdays: a song and then, in the last lesson of the day, cakes.

It was three-thirty at last. Mum was waiting eagerly for Tilly at the school gate.

"Did you have a good day?" asked Mum.

"Great thanks, Mum. Can't wait for my party."

Mum smiled. She was looking forward to the party too. She'd taken the evening off work especially to be there. "There's a big surprise waiting for you at home, which is going to make your day even better," she said.

Opening the front door to their little house, Tilly was aware of laughter. You know the sort – belly laughter that brings tears to your eyes. Sitting in the living room with Grammy and Poppa Millpepper was Tilly's Uncle Leonardo, her dad's older brother.

"Tilly! My you've grown!" Uncle Leonardo bellowed, his enormous voice echoing through the room. "Come here and give your old uncle a big hug."

Uncle Leonardo was an adventurer who had

been around the world at least three times. He was slightly taller and definitely broader than his brother, but had the same curly, auburn hair. However, unlike her dad who was clean-shaven, Uncle Leonardo sported an impressive red beard which covered his entire face. To Tilly, he was the most exciting human she had ever known, and the fact he was her uncle, well, she couldn't be prouder. He was always full of stories of his adventures, exciting stories of the places he had visited and the people he had met. It had been Uncle Leonardo who had started her hat collection on her fifth birthday, with an Australian cork hat he had purchased from a sheep farmer in the Australian Outback. Tilly had immediately fallen in love with the huge chocolate brown hat, with its corks dangling from its wide brim, and decided there and then that she would be an adventurer too... when she was old enough.

"Uncle Leo, you said you'd be here my birthday and you are!" cried Tilly, throwing her arms around him. "How long are you staying?"

"Until the end of the week and then I'm off to South America again."

"In search of that lost tribe?"

"Yes, well remembered. I hope this time I'll be lucky enough to find them." Uncle Leonardo's eyes seemed to twinkle as he took out a small parcel from his backpack. In a low voice, so no one else in the room could hear, he said, "I found this decorated stone in a market place in India. The man who sold it to me said it's a wishing stone. I don't know how true it is, though," he admitted. "But I thought you might like to have it."

Tilly unwrapped the little parcel and stared down at the smooth, flat, yellow stone. On one side was a painting of a red flower and on the other a tiger with enormous paws.

"Thank you, Uncle Leo. Do you think it will help me in my maths test tomorrow?"

Uncle Leonardo threw his head back and

laughed. "To be honest, Tilly, I would be very surprised if it had any sort of powers. I think you should just look on it as a pretty ornament from India." Tilly couldn't help but notice that a mischievous look had appeared in his eyes. "But just in case," he whispered, "be careful. Apparently, it only grants three wishes."

Just then the doorbell rang and Tilly's friends started to arrive. Placing the stone in her back pocket, she put it out of her mind for the time being.

It was a lovely party with games and plenty of delicious food. Eventually it was time for Tilly to cut her birthday cake, which Mum had baked and iced into the shape of a skateboard.

"Make a wish, Tilly!" everyone cried.

Tilly took a deep breath. She had been thinking long and hard about her birthday wish for several days. Wishes she had made on previous birthdays had rarely come true, but it was always fun making them. This year, though, she wanted her wish to be special. After all, ten was a monumental age. It was the first time she was going to be a two-digit number. So, yes, this year was special. The week before, Tilly had watched a TV programme about a woman trying to teach a chimpanzee sign language. She had thought how wonderful it would be to be able to talk to animals, just like

Doctor Doolittle. OK, deep down she knew it was a crazy idea, but it was her birthday and so that was her wish.

She closed her eyes tightly and at the same time she slipped her hand into her pocket and felt for the smooth, yellow stone. Perhaps, with the added power of the Wishing Stone, this year her wish might just come true.

CHAPTER 3

The Letter

SADLY BY the following Saturday Tilly's birthday wish still hadn't come true. She kept talking to Jellicle, but disappointingly the little cat was still not talking back to her. Of course, she wasn't really surprised, but she did think that if Uncle Leonardo ever went back to India he should ask for his money back on the Wishing Stone! He'd left yesterday for South America, and the Millpepper household was now returning to normal.

Weekends in the Millpepper households, unlike weekdays, were a time for everyone to do whatever they liked.

Dad devoted most of his time to his hobby of woodcraft, making things like small model figures or, sometimes, pieces of furniture. When he wasn't in his workshop at the bottom of the garden he'd be in the kitchen, probably making his signature dish of spaghetti and meatballs, which everyone agreed was delicious.

Mum would spend her free time catching up with her friends, or swimming or doing Pilates. She also enjoyed Grammy's company and catching up with the soaps.

Standing less than five-feet tall in her fluffy slippers, grey-eyed Grammy was pink-faced with silver hair. She always wore elasticated trousers, because, as she put it, *"These days I wear clothes for comfort. You will too when you get to my age."* She enjoyed knitting – knitting whilst sitting in the winged-backed chair by her front room window watching passers-by. She and Poppa had lived in their terraced house with its purple front door for over forty years, and she couldn't ever imagine moving from the street.

Poppa had an allotment nearby, where he grew

fruit and vegetables. Every day – come rain or shine, weekday or weekend – he would wander down there, where he would sit and chat to his friends, drinking tea from a flask and eating cheese and pickle sandwiches under an enormous apple tree. Poppa, like Tilly, collected hats – he needed his hats to keep his rapidly balding head warm. He was a jolly fellow and his large waistline wobbled as he laughed, and he did laugh a lot. That was one of the reasons why every Christmas he would put on a red suit to play the part of Father Christmas in a local store.

Tilly, on the other hand, liked to spend her free time at the skatepark or in the garden, climbing the only tree: a large oak planted more than a century ago. She could sit for hours on end on one of its branches simply thinking or reading a book and occasionally spying on her brother on his computer in his bedroom.

Yes, weekends in both numbers 16 and 18 Park Street were usually very relaxed and peaceful.

The postman always came later on Saturdays, and it was no different on this particular Saturday.

It was mid-morning. Grammy had just popped round for a chat with Mum. They were sitting at the kitchen table drinking tea and dunking the occasional chocolate biscuit. Dad was in his shed. Bradley was up in his room with his headphones on, playing on his computer, totally unaware of what was going on in the rest of the house. Tilly, having fed Jellicle, was now busy polishing her skateboard, getting it ready to go to the skatepark where she had arranged to meet Leila.

The letterbox at the front door rattled loudly.

Picking up the post from the doormat, Mum sifted quickly through the mound of mail, which consisted of mostly flyers and nasty brown envelopes containing bills. However, a large white envelope addressed to her caught her eye. She turned it over and was surprised to see it had a return address for a solicitor on the back.

Why would a solicitor be writing to her? she wondered.

Returning to the kitchen, she sat down at the table opposite Grammy and stared at the envelope.

"It's from a solicitor," she said softly, holding up the envelope so Grammy could see. "Why would a solicitor be writing to me?"

"Oh, my dear! How worrying," declared Grammy, her face looking more pink than usual.

"Would you like me to open it? In my experience of solicitor's letters, it's never good news."

"No, no, it's OK," replied Mum, taking a quick sip of tea from her mug. With her hand shaking slightly, she slowly slit open the envelope and pulled out the letter from inside. Without a word to Grammy, she began to read it quietly to herself. Suddenly she let out an ear-splitting scream, which almost made Grammy fall off her chair. The scream was so loud that even Dad heard her from his workshop and came rushing into the kitchen, thinking his wife must be hurt.

Dropping her skateboard, Tilly appeared beside her dad.

All three of them were now staring at Mum.

"Grammy, you were right. It is bad news!" Tears were welling in Mum's eyes. "My Great Aunt Phoebe has died!" She dabbed her cheeks with a tissue, then waved the letter in the air. "But she's only gone and left me her house in the country!"

"Wow!" they all cried.

"I didn't even know you had a Great Aunt Phoebe," added Dad.

"No, you wouldn't, Archie. You've never met her. She was quite a strange woman and didn't really get on with the rest of my family, but I liked her. I liked her a lot. When I was a child, I used to stay with her sometimes during the summer holidays, whilst my parents went off abroad on one of their 'driving tours'. She was married to a man called Frank Kendal – at least, I think that was his name. Only he died when I was very little. They never had any children. I remember thinking it was quite sad that they didn't... I can't believe she's left me Dingleby Hall!"

"Dingleby Hall? It sounds very grand," replied Dad.

"Yes, it is," answered Mum, reading the letter again. "There's only one problem, though ... We have to live there!"

"What?" they all chorused.

"For a year," Mum continued. "If I want to inherit Dingleby Hall, the letter says, we have to live there for a whole year!"

CHAPTER 4

Moving

THE NEWS that they might have to move out of London to Essex and leave everything they knew and loved behind for a year began a big debate within the Millpepper household.

Mum thought it was well worth taking what she called 'a career break' for. Dad didn't want to leave his job at all.

"And I simply can't commute that distance for a whole year!" exclaimed Dad.

"A year will fly by," insisted Mum. "It's a lovely place, and we'd have so much space. Grammy, there are even enough rooms for you and Poppa, if you wanted to come with us."

"You can count me and Poppa out," sniffed Grammy. "I'm never leaving London! You do know – don't you? – that they don't have shops in the countryside."

"What about school?" cried Tilly. "It'll be too far to travel by bus every day, and there are cows and sheep in the country, aren't there? Think of the smell."

Right in the middle of their discussion, Poppa arrived with a bag full of new potatoes from his allotment. So, Mum had to read the letter to him all over again, which restarted the debate.

Sitting down at the kitchen table, Poppa let out an enormous sigh. "OK, I've listened to all your arguments. Now let me tell you what I think," he said, taking hold of Mum's hand. "What a kind and generous person your great-aunt must have been, Wendy, to have left you the place you spent such happy summers in as a child."

"Archie," he continued, turning to his son, "if you explain it to them, your company might say you can work from home for most of the week. A lot of people do these days."

"Tilly, my dear Tilly," – he turned to his granddaughter – "you and Bradley will have to change schools, I'm afraid. Yes, there are animals other than cats and dogs in the countryside, but it's a wonderful place where the air is almost free from exhaust fumes. Now, my darling wife, we're at the time of our lives where there is not much to look forward to. Think of it as an adventure for all of us. It will be something we'll be able to talk about for years to come, and of course there are shops! So, everyone, I think we should take up the challenge and move to the countryside as one big happy family. After all, it's only for a year. Discussion over. Now I could do with a cup of tea."

No one argued with Poppa's reasoning because everything he said was right. So, the decision was made, just like that. The news that they were leaving London came as a big shock to Bradley, who appeared bleary-eyed in the kitchen a few hours later. Surprisingly though, he didn't create too much of a fuss. As long as he could take his computer with him, he was happy.

Before the end of July, all the arrangements for their move were in place. They even hired a removal company to take all of their things there that they couldn't bear to leave behind.

Finally, the day arrived. It was time for the family to go. Grammy was the one who shed the most tears as they bundled into the large people carrier Dad had bought the week before. Living in London, the family hadn't needed their own transport. However, now they were moving to the countryside, they decided they would need to have a car.

Placing Jellicle in her cat carrier securely on the back seat of the car, Tilly sat beside her and buckled up. As their neighbours and friends waved them off, Leila passed a note to Tilly through the car window.

"It's my address, just in case you forget."

"I won't forget," laughed Tilly. "Anyway, you

and your mum are coming to stay in a few weeks, remember."

＊ ＊ ＊

An hour and a half of motorway later, the roads in front of them became twisty and narrow, with high hedges and the occasional gate. Driving through the picturesque village of Little Abbot, they passed a primary school.

"Look Tilly, that's your new school," pointed out Mum.

Tilly gazed from the car window. The school buildings looked ancient.

"I won't know anyone, Mum," Tilly said gloomily.

"Oh Tilly, I'm sure you'll soon make new friends, you'll see. You'll be fine."

Leaving the village behind them, the roads seemed to get even narrower. Then at last Mum shouted, "Here's the turning! I remember that house on the corner. Yes, this is definitely the turning."

Manoeuvring the car along an unkempt lane, they passed several other houses on the way before the track finally came to an abrupt end. Dad brought the car to a stop in front of a large wooden gate. Mum got out and lifted the metal bar to open it. The sound of stones on the gravel driveway crunching beneath the car wheels encouraged Dad to drive slowly. After all, he didn't want to damage the paintwork of their new car. Passing through an avenue of densely planted trees, they all began to wonder if they were going in the right direction. Then, as they rounded a bend, the vegetation dropped away and in front of them, rising amid its vast grounds, was the magnificent Dingleby Hall.

CHAPTER 5

Dingleby Hall

DINGLEBY HALL was a large, red brick building with four separate chimney pots on its roof. Its facade was adorned with vibrant bundles of purple wisteria clinging to wall-mounted trellises.

They drove up to the front door, and everyone got out, except for Jellicle, who was fast asleep in her carrier.

"Cor, it certainly is a big place!" exclaimed Dad, standing back to count the windows.

"Mum, look!" yelled Tilly. "The door's opening!"

Sure enough, the dark blue front door opened and a tall woman, dressed from head to toe in green, stepped out of the doorway. Immediately,

Tilly stood nervously behind Mum. From her hiding place, she peaked out at the scary looking woman.

"You must be the Millpeppers," the woman began. Holding out her hand, she took a step towards Mum. "I'm Sybil Heliot. I've been looking after the house since Mrs Kendal's sad passing. Welcome to Dingleby Hall."

Sybil Heliot was one of those individuals who different people would notice different things about her when they looked at her for the first time. For Mum, it was Sybil Heliot's raven black, straight hair, but for Dad, it was the length of Sybil Heliot's nose. Poppa thought her piercingly green eyes reminded him of a cat. Grammy believed the woman could do with a bit of foundation and blusher to improve her grey almost translucent skin. Bradley? Well, he had hardly noticed her at all. His eyes, as always, were on his iPhone. Tilly, however, noticed everything about Sybil Heliot and the only conclusion she came up with was that she was a witch! Not that she had ever knowingly met one before, but the evidence was standing in front of her. The woman only needed a black, pointy hat to complete the picture.

Mum moved closer, with Tilly still hiding behind her. Although somewhat taken aback, like the rest of the family, at Sybil Heliot's appearance, Mum extended her arm and shook her bony hand.

"Pleased to meet you. The solicitor explained

that you were still employed here. You live nearby, I understand?"

"Yes, with my daughter Bella," she said, her green eyes seeking out Tilly. "Bella must be about the same age as your little… kitten."

"Come on, Tilly," encouraged Mum, trying to coax Tilly out from behind her. "Say hello to Mrs Heliot."

"Hello," said Tilly, without looking the woman in the eye, in case she cast a spell on her. Sybil Heliot simply forced a smile through her thin lips. Tilly wondered if she had any teeth missing.

"It's Ms Heliot, by the way," insisted Sybil Heliot. "Would you like me to show you around the house?"

"Yes thanks, that's a good idea," piped up Dad.

"Can I get Jelly out of the car first, Dad?" asked Tilly.

"Jelly?" enquired Sybil Heliot, holding her long nose in the air as if she could smell something nasty.

"Jelly's real name is Jellicle. She's my cat," said Tilly firmly.

"I see," replied Sybil Heliot. "I have to say cats are my favourite animal. I have several beautiful specimens of my own. I hope she gets on with dogs, though, because there is a nasty, smelly hound in residence. His name is Dexter, and he's not keen on cats."

"I'm sure Jelly will be fine, as long as Dexter doesn't chase her," insisted Tilly. "Anyway, I'll keep her in my bedroom while she gets used to her new home."

"Probably a good idea," replied Sybil Heliot. "We don't want Jellicle to come to any harm now, do we?"

Tilly decided there and then that she definitely didn't like the witch-like Sybil Heliot.

Entering Dingleby Hall, the family's first view was of a sweeping staircase which dominated the large blue and red tiled hallway. There were numerous inviting doors surrounding it, just waiting to be opened. While Tilly and Bradley ran eagerly from room to room, shrieking with delight at what they were finding, the grown-ups followed at a more leisurely pace. Surprisingly, none of the rooms had much furniture nor many knick-knacks in them. It was just as well they had decided not to leave their things behind in London.

On the first floor, there were eight bedrooms and four bathrooms – enough for the whole family with plenty of room for guests. Looking out of the window from the bedroom she had already bagged for herself, Tilly could see the removal van that had all their things in it chugging up the driveway towards the house.

"The removal van's arrived!" she shouted.

* * *

The removal men were taking a long time to unload all their things. Tilly was getting bored, so Mum told her she could go and explore the garden as long as she didn't go out of the gate.

Strolling back down the driveway, Tilly could hear voices. As she rounded the corner, she caught sight of a girl with light brown hair cut to her chin and a boy with dark tousled hair and braces on his teeth. They were both riding mountain bikes and were heading her way.

"Hi," the girl called out. "Are you moving in?"

"Yes," replied Tilly and then added, "Do you live around here?"

The children stopped in front of her and got off their bikes.

"I live with my mum in the grounds of Little Abbot Riding School," said the girl. "My name's Edie and this is my friend Felix. He lives in the village. What's your name?"

"It's Tilly," replied Tilly.

"Well, Tilly, we were just coming to check on Sam. It's usually my mum's job, but she's not well today, so I told her I'd do it."

"Sam?" asked Tilly.

"Yes, you know, Sam, Mrs Kendal's pony."

CHAPTER 6

Sam

THE NEWS that there was a pony somewhere on the property came as a big surprise to Tilly.

"Oh, I didn't know Dingleby Hall came with a pony and I'm sure my mum doesn't know either," she said. "We were told there's a dog called Dexter, but come to think of it, he's very quiet cause we've not heard or seen him either."

"That's because Dexter's been staying with us," pointed out Edie. "Ms Heliot's not keen on dogs and didn't want to be bothered with him. He was a rescue. Mrs Kendal was a very kind lady and was always rescuing animals. If she could, she would find them new homes, otherwise she kept them herself. Dexter and Sam are the only two animals she had left."

"I see. Well I've got a cat. I hope Dexter won't be nasty to her," said Tilly.

"If I know anything about cats," replied Felix, "Dexter will be frightened of her!"

Tilly laughed. "You're probably right. Jelly does like to get her claws out sometimes. OK, can you show me where the pony is?"

"Come this way," said Edie, as she and Felix started pushing their bikes up the drive towards the Hall.

They led Tilly towards the back of the building, where a large lawn took them to a wooden-fenced paddock. Standing in the far corner, with his back towards them, swishing his long black tail was Sam.

"He's a bit grumpy these days," pointed out Edie. "I think he misses Mrs Kendal. Do you ride, Tilly?"

"Me, no, I've never even been near a pony

before. He looks big."

"He's fourteen hands, which is how horses and ponies are measured, in hands."

"Oh, I see," said Tilly, having no clue what a 'hand' was, apart from the one on the end of her arm, of course. "Do you both ride?"

"Yes, a lot of people do around here. My mum actually owns and runs Little Abbot Riding School. These days, though, we have mostly livery horses. If you want me to ask her, I'm sure she would come to the Hall and give you some riding lessons and show you how to look after him."

"I'm not sure…" replied Tilly rather hesitantly, wondering at the same time what a livery horse was.

"No pressure. Come on, let's go and meet your pony."

Walking around the perimeter of the paddock, they finally reached the area where Sam was standing beneath the overhanging branches of an enormous tree. He was a handsome boy, with big brown eyes that had sadness about them. His coat was mainly a very rich brown and there were large blobs of white dotted about here and there. He snorted as the children approached.

"Hello Sam, we've brought your new owner to meet you," declared Edie.

Swishing his tail even harder, he snorted again.

"Why don't you stroke his neck," suggested Felix. "He'll like that."

Nervously, Tilly stepped forward and stretched out her hand. His coat was warm and surprisingly soft. Sam turned his head and looked at her and snorted for a third time.

"Perhaps I should learn to ride him," pondered Tilly, "if my mum and dad agree, that is. Does he have a saddle and the other stuff he needs?"

"Of course," answered Edie. "Behind those trees over there are a couple of stables, a tack room and another paddock with an area for training and jumping. Come on I'll show you."

The small tack room smelt of leather. There

were several saddles of various sizes and bridles hanging from one of the walls.

"Mrs Kendal used to have three ponies, but sadly two of them died from old age. Then, of course, there was Willow, the donkey. Ms Heliot got rid of her when Mrs Kendal died. Apparently, she couldn't stand Willow's braying."

"That's so sad… What are these?" asked Tilly,

picking up some red and blue ribbons.

"Rosettes," replied Felix. "The ponies used to go in for Pony Club competitions. Of course, Mrs Kendal didn't ride them, but she encouraged children from the village who couldn't afford to have riding lessons to come up here. She taught them how to ride and to look after the ponies."

"I see. That was nice of her. Who's this, one of the children from the village?" queried Tilly, pointing to one of several pictures pinned to the wall. It was of a girl, with a face like thunder, sitting on a grey pony.

"No, that's Bella, Ms Heliot's daughter. She thinks she's the bee's knees when it comes to riding. That picture was taken at Easter when she didn't get a rosette. That's why she looks so angry," grinned Edie.

"Interesting," said Tilly. "I've met Ms Heliot. She's a scary woman."

"Yes, most kids around here are terrified of her, because she looks like..."

"A witch?" suggested Tilly, finishing Edie's sentence.

"Yes," her two new friends replied, "a witch!"

CHAPTER 7

A Midnight Surprise

RETURNING TO the front of the house, Tilly waved Edie and Felix goodbye, promising to get in touch as soon as possible about the riding lessons. She noticed that the removal van had left and ran inside to find her parents to tell them about Sam and Dexter. Her mum and Grammy were in the kitchen preparing dinner when Tilly burst in.

"Mum!" cried Tilly. "I've already made two new friends, and guess what? We've got a pony!"

Mum, who was standing at the kitchen sink peeling potatoes, stopped what she was doing and turned and stared at Tilly.

"I remember now my mother telling me that aunty had started taking in abandoned animals. I'd quite forgotten. Well, well, a pony, whatever next."

After dinner, with great excitement, they all went out to the paddock to meet Sam. Leaning over the fence, Dad couldn't help pointing out what everyone else was thinking.

"None of us know anything about horses. Perhaps we should try to find him another home?"

"Maybe Dad's right, Tilly," added Mum. "He might be happier with people who know what they're doing."

"No, we can't get rid of him!" wailed Tilly. "Aunty rescued him, and this is where he should be. Please, it's up to us to take care of him. If you give Edie's mum a ring, she'll come and tell us all we need to know about looking after him and teach me how to ride. I really want to learn. Anyway, Edie's family have been looking after Dexter for months. It's time he came home."

"I'm sure your aunt would have expected us to

take care of him, Wendy," said Poppa.

"And what happens to him next year, when we leave to go back to London?" asked Dad.

"We'll cross that bridge when we come to it," replied Poppa. "In the meantime, let's go and wander over to the stables and have a look round. This whole estate is going to take us a while to explore, and I can't wait to get started. Come on, Brad my boy, you can lead the way."

"You all go on ahead. I'll follow you later," said Grammy. "The poor animal looks so sad. I'll go back in the house and get him a carrot. That's something I do know about horses – they love carrots."

It had been an exhausting day and it was now time for bed. There were boxes of the family's things stacked everywhere throughout the house, and Tilly's bedroom was no exception. However, because her room was more than four times bigger than the one she had in London, there was plenty of space for everything. She even had a walk-in wardrobe for all her clothes and hats.

Jellicle had been happy enough since she'd been let out of her carrier. She'd been spending her time playing hide-and-seek around the boxes, jumping occasionally at shadows and then stopping to give her paws a lick.

"You'll have to stay in here a few days, Jelly, and then you can roam round the rest of the house. You'll love the garden. There's so many trees for both of us to climb." Tilly hesitated. "You won't be the only animal in the house, though, Jelly. I'm sorry but you're going to have to share it with a dog."

The news that she was going to have to live with a dog didn't seem to worry Jellicle one bit. She just carried on licking herself. Tilly climbed onto her bed, and as she slipped under her duvet cover, Mum appeared in her bedroom.

"I've just got off the phone to Mrs Westbury, Edie's mum. She said she would bring Dexter up to the Hall sometime tomorrow. She'll also talk to us about looking after Sam, and if you want, she'll give you a riding lesson. Where's Jellicle, by the way?" asked Mum, looking round the room.

"Exploring. I don't want to let her out of the room yet, in case she gets scared and runs away... Thanks, Mum, for bringing us here. It's turning out to be quite fun."

Mum smiled. "I'm pleased you're happy. I'm guessing it helped making friends on your first day. Your brother's happy too. He and Dad have just managed to connect his computer. Goodnight sweetheart, sleep well," she said, bending down and kissing Tilly's forehead.

The minute Mum left the room, Jellicle jumped up on to Tilly's bed and settled down for the night. Pulling the covers up to her chin, Tilly fell instantly into a deep sleep. Maybe that's why she wasn't sure if she was dreaming or not when, as the grandfather clock downstairs struck midnight, her bedroom was suddenly filled with a blinding light. As her eyes adjusted to the glare, she could see Jellicle was awake too and was staring in the direction of her chest of drawers. Climbing out of bed, Tilly moved cautiously towards it and pulled open the top drawer. Immediately she was stunned to realise that the yellow light was coming from the tiger's eyes on the Wishing Stone.

CHAPTER 8

Learning to Ride

TILLY WOKE early the next morning and rubbed her eyes. Had she imagined it? Had there been a bright light last night coming from the Wishing Stone? Throwing off her bed covers, she climbed out of bed and moved cautiously towards her chest of drawers and pulled open the top drawer. There it was, tucked right at the back: the decorated yellow stone. There certainly wasn't a light coming from it now. It must have been a dream, after all. Mustn't it?

Tilly was the last one down to breakfast, where she found her entire family buzzing with excitement about the day ahead. Dad was excited because he had discovered not one but two outside buildings, one of which he could use for his workshop. Poppa was also excited, because there was an orchard of apple and plum trees, together with several large raised beds for him to grow his vegetables, alongside a very impressive greenhouse. To cap it all, in one of the outbuildings they had found a ride-on mower. Bradley had already volunteered to mow the lawns and couldn't wait to start the engine. However, as Mum pointed out, there were a number of containers to unpack first, and she expected everyone to help. Without complaining, after breakfast, they all got to work on the downstairs boxes.

Coming from their compact terraced houses in London, they were all in awe at the size of Dingleby Hall. As well as the spacious kitchen, which was big enough for a table and a sofa, there were several other large rooms downstairs to fill. It was agreed that Grammy and Poppa should have their own sitting room, somewhere they could have some peace and quiet. Since there were three generous-size reception rooms to choose from, that didn't prove a problem. There was also a good-size study for Dad for when he started working from home – after his two weeks holiday – and a dining room for them all to come together at the end of the day. So, everyone was happy.

The unpacking occupied them for a few hours and it was soon lunchtime. The family – apart from Dad who was still sorting things out in his study – were in the kitchen together enjoying a meal of salads and cold meats

"What time do you expect Sybil Heliot, Wendy?" asked Poppa.

Mum looked up at the clock on the wall.

"We agreed she would start about two. She's going to clean every weekday afternoon for a couple of hours, as she has been doing. I know she's a bit unusual, but we need her at the moment."

"I know we do, Wendy," began Grammy, lowering her voice, "but there is definitely something very odd about her. You must see it. I mean, I'm sure she can't help it, but she looks…" – Grammy glanced over at Tilly. She was trying her best not to say the word 'witch' in front of her granddaughter – "… magical, and if I'm not very much mistaken, she seems to be looking for something."

"Of course, she's not 'magical'! I mean, if she was, she would just wave a wand and the whole house would be clean," mused Mum, trying to raise a smile. "As for her looking for something, I think she just likes to do a thorough job, that's all."

Tilly sat listening attentively. Was she hearing right? Did Grammy think Sybil Heliot was a witch too?

"Mum," she began, "do you think she's a witch?"

Mum looked furiously at Grammy before answering her daughter.

"Of course not, darling, witches – the ones

you're picturing – are only for story books. Grammy shouldn't be putting these notions into your head. Ms Heliot is a mother like me. So, no more talk of witches or magic. Alright?"

"But, Mum, I think she's a witch and so do the children in the village…"

"I said no more talk of witches, Tilly!" said Mum sternly, bringing the whole conversation to a close.

When they had finished lunch, Poppa glanced out of one of the front windows. He could see Sybil Heliot puffing towards the Hall on her ancient bicycle. With every turn of the pedals, the metal pushbike clanked loudly, almost as if it was announcing its arrival. Opening the door, Poppa greeted Sybil Heliot before returning quickly to the kitchen.

"She's here!" revealed Poppa, picking up his cap and placing it firmly on his head. "I'm going outside to get out of that woman's way. Witch or no witch, you can say what you like, Wendy, but I think Grammy's right about her looking for something. I caught her on her hands and knees yesterday with a torch peeping through the floorboards. You can't tell me she was looking for more dust! Anyway, Bradley, do you fancy helping me in the garden? I thought we could try to get that mower started."

Immediately, Bradley put his phone down on the table. He didn't need to be asked twice. Jumping up from his chair, his face broke out into a grin with the thought of the ride on mower. Mum smiled. It was so nice to see her son excited by something other than his computer.

At that exact moment, the trill of the old-fashioned phone in the hall rang out. It was Mrs Westbury. She had rung to tell Mum that she had a few hours to spare and would it be convenient to bring Dexter up to the Hall now and, perhaps, give Tilly a riding lesson? Mum couldn't say no, so, just after three o'clock, Mrs Westbury pulled up to the front door in her green Land Rover.

Dexter, a brown and white Beagle with long floppy ears, was obviously delighted to be home. Springing down from the vehicle, he dashed around the garden with his nose to the ground. Then, spying Tilly at the front door, the little dog scampered up the three stone steps and leapt at the startled Tilly. With his tail wagging with excitement, he licked her with his wet tongue.

"Down Dexter! Down boy!" bellowed Mrs Westbury.

Obeying her command, Dexter stopped leaping up at Tilly and dashed through the open door into the hallway. It was just as well Jellicle was safely shut in her bedroom, thought Tilly. In the excitable mood Dexter was in, he would probably cause Jellicle to scramble up the nearest curtain in fright.

"Sorry about that. He's simply happy to be home," explained Mrs Westbury, who was a blond woman with a kind face and laughing eyes. Tilly liked her straightaway. She was dressed in a pair of beige jodhpurs and on her feet were black riding boots. In her left hand she was holding a black riding hat. "You must be Tilly," she said. "Edie's told me all about you. Are you ready for your first riding lesson? I've brought a hard hat for you to wear."

"Yes, thank you. I can't wait. I'll just go and tell Mum and Dad you're here, because they wanted to come along too. Mind you, I'm guessing they probably already know you've arrived, with Dexter tearing around the house."

While Mrs Westbury waited for Tilly, the figure of Sybil Heliot appeared in front of her, clearly taking her by surprise.

"Ms Heliot, you still work here, then?"

"Yes obviously, not that it's any of your business," snapped Sybil Heliot. Her sharp words caused Mrs Westbury's face to turn a deep shade of red. "How are my daughter's riding lessons going?" Sybil Heliot continued. "I expect her to win all her competitions this year."

"Bella is doing quite well."

"Only quite!" snarled Sybil Heliot, drawing herself up to her full height. "I expect you, Mrs Westbury, to turn her into a champion!"

Turning on her heels, Sybil Heliot marched back into the house.

✳ ✳ ✳

Dexter joined the family as they made their way to Sam's paddock. The young dog was still full of energy, and Bradley kept throwing a stick for him, which Dexter brought back quickly every time. Arriving at the field, Tilly could see that Sam was standing in exactly the same spot as yesterday.

"It's very good of you to give up your time to help us with the pony Mrs Westbury," said Mum.

"Believe me, it's no trouble at all, and please call me Jo. 'Mrs Westbury' makes me feel old... You see, I owe Mrs Kendall a lot. She was very good to me. In fact, if it wasn't for her, I wouldn't have learned to ride and I certainly wouldn't be running my own riding school. I was one of the children from the village who used to come up here and ride Mrs Kendall's ponies. I'll always be very grateful to her for giving me the opportunity. Right, Tilly, let's go and get Sam's tack and cleaning brushes, then I'll show you how to groom and saddle him."

Tilly didn't realise how much effort went into grooming a horse and how many different brushes were involved. A good half an hour later, Sam was finally gleaming from head to toe from all the cleaning. He was now ready for his tack. Listening carefully to the instructions Jo was giving her, Tilly eventually had Sam's bridle and saddle in place.

"OK, we'll make our way to the training ring. Take his reins, Tilly. You can lead him."

As her parents and Jo walked ahead with Dexter at their heels, Tilly walked alongside Sam.

"That dog never shuts up," said a voice.

"Sorry?" said Tilly, stopping and looking around, expecting to see someone behind her. But there was nobody there. She must have imagined it.

Arriving at the training ring, Jo pulled down the stirrups and showed Tilly how to mount using a mounting block.

"Right, your turn, Tilly. First of all, always check the girth before getting into the saddle. I've seen many a rider come unstuck by a loose girth."

Tilly looked at Jo quizzically

"OK, the strap under his belly, holding the saddle on," explained Jo. "Now stand on the mounting block. That's right. Even if the girth is tight, most riders use a mounting block these days or whatever's around they can stand on. This helps to prevent the saddle from being pulled over, a movement which could potentially hurt the pony's back. Reins in your left hand and with the same hand, hold onto the pommel of the saddle. Well done. Now turn to face your pony's tail. Take the stirrup in your right hand. Put your left foot in the stirrup, and then with a small spring, swing yourself into the saddle. Excellent, that wasn't too difficult, was it?" she asked, as Tilly sat triumphantly in the saddle for the first time.

"Wow, this is great," cried Tilly. "Just like climbing a tree."

Jo smiled. "I've got a feeling you're going to be a natural. Right, place your other foot in the stirrup, and then I'll lead you around for a bit. If you feel confident, we'll have a trot. Sam is very good. He's used to having non-riders on his back."

Tilly and her parents had a lovely afternoon. Even Dad felt brave enough to have a go, although his legs were a little too long for the stirrups. After riding Sam back to his field, Tilly dismounted and Jo showed her how to remove his tack.

"Why don't you take his bridle and saddle back to the tack room, Tilly? We'll walk back with Jo to her car," said Mum.

"OK Mum. Thanks, Jo, it was very kind of you to give me a riding lesson," said Tilly.

"It was my pleasure, Tilly. I'll send Edie up here tomorrow. She's got her own pony and often helps out at the riding school. I'm quite confident you'll be safe in her hands. By the way, you might want to get some basic riding clothes, jodhpurs, boots, and a riding hat of course, just to start you off."

Reaching her vehicle, Jo turned to Mum and Dad.

"Look, I have to say this. Be careful of Sybil Heliot. She's a peculiar woman. I personally wouldn't trust her."

Mum and Dad waved to her as her Land Rover made its way down the drive.

"Someone else who's not a fan of Sybil Heliot!" exclaimed Mum.

"Well, to be honest," began Dad, "there is something about the woman I'm not comfortable about either. For one thing she always seems to be looking over my shoulder."

"Don't tell me you think she's a witch too?"

Dad stared at Mum. "Well, I didn't before, but come to think of it…"

✳ ✳ ✳

After closing the door to the tack room, Tilly made her way back to Sam, who had already positioned himself in his favourite corner of the paddock. Tilly reached up and stroked his neck.

"Thank you for letting me ride you today, Sam. I really enjoyed it," said Tilly.

"You're welcome," replied Sam.

CHAPTER 9

A Bizarre Conversation

TILLY STOOD staring at Sam. Sam turned his head and stared at Tilly.

"Did you… just speak… to me?" she stuttered.

Sam snorted. "It's as much as a surprise to me," he replied.

"Oh my goodness!" cried Tilly. Taking several steps backwards, she lost her footing and toppled to the ground. "My wish, the Wishing Stone has granted my wish!"

"I've no idea what you're talking about," answered Sam.

"But why," continued Tilly, talking out loud to herself, "can I only talk to you, not Jelly or Dexter?"

"Whose Jelly?"

Tilly scrambled to her feet and brushed the dirt off her jeans.

"Sorry, Jellicle my cat. I'll introduce you eventually. Wow, this is unbelievable! Leila will not believe me!"

"And Leila is?"

"My best friend."

Sam snorted. "I had a best friend once. I miss her."

Tilly stepped closer to him and looked directly into his eyes.

"Is that why you look so sad? Because that's the first thing I noticed about you, the fact you look so sad. Was your best friend one of the rescue horses that died?"

Sam shook his head. "No, she was taken away by that evil monster."

"Are you talking about Ms Heliot? Was the donkey your best friend?"

"Yes. Willow and I were both foals together in Ireland before coming over here. I miss her so much." He lowered his head.

"I'm so sorry," said Tilly, stroking his neck. "Do you know what happened to her?"

"No, I wish I did. A man I've never seen before came to the field one day with the monster and took her away. I've not seen her since."

"That's awful. Maybe I can find out where he took her. If it helps, I'm not a fan of Ms Heliot either. She scares me."

Sam snorted and shook his head up and down.

"I like you."

"I like you too, Sam. Look, I'm going to have to go in. I can see my brother walking towards us. I'm guessing dinner's ready. Can I get you anything before I go?"

"No thanks, I'm fine. It's quite something isn't it, that we can talk to each other?"

"Yes, Sam, it's quite something." Tilly threw her arms around his neck and hugged him. Perhaps, she thought, the reason the Wishing Stone granted her wish was so she could help him. "I think," she whispered close to his ear so her brother couldn't hear, "we should keep the fact we can talk to each other a secret, at least for now."

Sam threw his head up and down again in agreement.

The following morning, a parcel arrived. It contained a pair of dark blue jodhpurs, black riding boots and a blue riding hat – all ordered the day before from the internet.

With the sun streaming through the gap in her

curtain, Tilly was already up and dressed in her brand-new riding clothes.

"Are you going out to see the pony already?" asked Mum, as Tilly appeared in the kitchen.

"Yes, I thought I'd go and groom him before Edie gets here."

"Well, just be careful," said Dad, peering over the top of his newspaper, "and remember what Jo said about not standing behind him. His back legs are very powerful. They could give you a nasty kick... Perhaps Brad should go with you?"

Seeing her brother's face drop at the thought of having to 'childmind' her, Tilly said, "Don't worry I'll be fine, Dad, I promise. I won't go anywhere near his back legs."

* * *

Sam was standing in his favourite place, but the minute he saw Tilly approaching, he let out an enormous whinny and trotted over to her.

"It's good to see you too," said Tilly. Reaching

up towards him, she stroked the pony's nose.

"I see you're ready for riding in your new clothes," said Sam.

Tilly smiled, "Yes, and I've even got a brand-new hat. I collect hats, so this is a great addition. I'll just go and get the brushes and give you a good clean."

"Do you want a lift to the top of the field?"

"Without a saddle?"

"Yes, bareback," said Sam and immediately knelt down on his front legs. "Jump on."

It was the oddest thing to be riding Sam, not only without a saddle, but also with only his mane to hold onto. Nevertheless, Tilly loved it. Jumping off him when they reached the far fence, Tilly ran to the tack room and came back with everything she needed. She spent a long time brushing and talking to him before Edie arrived with Felix in tow.

"Morning Tilly. Cor, Sam is looking smart. Mum said you did very well yesterday. Are you ready for your next lesson? I thought we'd use the lunging rein." Tilly looked puzzled. All these new words she had to learn. "Come on, let's get his tack on and I'll show you what I mean. Love the jodhpurs, by the way, very smart."

As Tilly put on Sam's bridle and saddle under the watchful eye of Edie, Tilly asked, "Edie, do you know what happened to the donkey that lived here?"

"Ms Heliot told my mum she sold her to a man who does donkey rides at the seaside."

So, thought Tilly, all I have to do now is find out which seaside. The only way I'm going to do that is by asking Sybil Heliot. The prospect of actually having a conversation with her sent shivers through Tilly. But, if she were ever going to be an adventurer, she would have to get used to overcoming her fears. She just hoped Sybil Heliot didn't cast a spell on her!

CHAPTER 10

The Photo Album

IT WOULD be true to say that on their first meeting Dexter and Jellicle had been rather surprised at encountering each other. Letting her out of her bedroom after a long couple of days, Tilly had watched nervously as her little cat had descended the stairs. Stopping occasionally, Jellicle seemed to be taking in her surroundings. Then moving slowly across the floor in the hallway, Jellicle's confidence had begun to return, until... Dexter, who had been sleeping in his basket dreaming of the rabbit he had chased the day before, suddenly woke up. His strong sense of smell and excellent hearing told him there was an intruder in the house. Leaping from his basket, the nails on his paws created a clicking sound as he raced into the hallway. That's where he came face to face with Jellicle. Skidding across the floor, he managed to halt in front of the terrified cat, whose hackles were now raised. Backing away from the spitting and hissing, Dexter crouched down. For once, his tail was not wagging. He was pondering what his next move should be.

It was Tilly who had come to the rescue. "OK you two," she had said, "you've got to learn to get along." Lowering her voice she added. "Now if I could talk to you like I can talk to Sam, we could sort all this out much quicker." She got down on the floor between the two animals. Jellicle immediately climbed onto her lap. "Dexter, this is Jellicle and if you play your cards right, I'm sure you could be great friends."

A few days later, Dexter and Jellicle were at least getting used to each other. Lying securely on a deep window ledge, Jellicle yawned. Stretching out her long legs she flicked the tip of her tail and gazed down at the panting dog looking eagerly up at her. He would have to wait. She was exhausted after all the rough and tumble of the last week and anyway it was way past her naptime.

✳ ✳ ✳

Tilly had been out riding every day for over a week now, and she was getting quite good. Jo had been right – she was a natural. She had mastered the rise to the trot and even managed to canter without falling off. It was because of her obvious skills that Edie suggested she accompany her to a horse show, which was being organised by the Little Abbot's Pony Club.

"You can come as my guest, but I definitely think you should join," said Edie, as she and Tilly rode their ponies along the country lanes. Edie's pony, Peter, was a blue roan half a hand smaller than Sam, and both ponies seemed to enjoy each other's company. "My mum runs it," Edie continued. "It's based at her riding school."

"What sort of things do you do? I mean, I

couldn't do any jumping or anything," pointed out Tilly.

"They wouldn't expect you to. A lot of the members are learning to ride and look after their ponies. There are prizes for the best-turned-out pony and rider and lots of games as well. The thing is, we've got a day ride coming up in a few weeks. If you're a member, you can come along if you want to. It's great fun. This year we're heading to the coast. We'll get to ride on the beach."

Sam pricked up his ears. Tilly instinctively knew what he was thinking.

"Do you think it's the beach where Willow gives rides?" asked Tilly.

"Hmm, I don't know. It could be, I guess. I thought you were going to ask Ms Heliot where the donkey went?"

Tilly ran her hand under Sam's mane.

"She's been away on holiday. She's back tomorrow."

"Oh yes, I'd forgotten they'd gone away for a

few days. I'm guessing Bella wants to get back for the horse show, so she can add to her collection of rosettes."

"I've not met her yet," said Tilly.

"You won't miss her. She'll be the one tearing about on her new pony, Orion. He's as black as night, and boy can he gallop and jump."

"Is Bella in the same class at school as you and Felix?"

"No, she doesn't go to school. She's taught at home, apparently. I think that's why she thinks she's better than everyone else."

Back at Sam's field, Tilly waved goodbye to Edie. Removing Sam's tack, Tilly asked him, "How do you feel about joining the Pony Club?"

Sam snorted. "Mrs Kendal was a member, so we ponies used to take part in shows and rides they organised… Do you think Willow might be at the beach where the Pony Club is going?"

"I don't know. Let's not get our hopes up. I'll talk to Ms Heliot, the minute she gets back."

＊ ＊ ＊

After dinner, the family went into the sitting room to watch television.

"Look what I found at the back of the cupboard in our bedroom, Archie," said Mum, "old photo albums. There're several pictures of me as a little girl. I must have been about Tilly's age."

They all gathered round Mum, intrigued to see old photographs of her and Aunt Phoebe.

"The rooms looked full of antiques in those days," pointed out Dad. "I wonder what happened to it all?"

"I guess Aunty got rid of her valuables as she got older. I especially remember that painting of Dingleby Hall," said Mum, pointing to a photo that showed the large painting in a gold frame hanging near the fireplace in the very room they were sitting. "Apparently it was painted by a local artist."

"You would have thought she would have kept

it for sentimental reasons, if nothing else," said Dad. "Looks like she liked to collect silver and porcelain objects. There's a lot in the photos."

"I must admit I was surprised how empty the rooms were when we arrived. I'm seeing the solicitor who dealt with her will next week. I'll ask him if he knows anything about them."

* * *

Sybil Heliot arrived at the Hall the following afternoon and got cracking on the cleaning. Still nervous in her presence, Tilly managed to pluck up the courage and ask her about Willow.

"Ms Heliot, I understand Sam used to share his field with a donkey?"

Sybil Heliot stopped her polishing and frowned.

"That noisy thing!" she muttered. "Have you ever heard a donkey bray? It goes straight through you. I'm sure Mrs Kendal was deaf."

"I see, hmm, what happened to the donkey?"

Sybil Heliot's eyes glared at Tilly.

"Why do you want to know?"

"I'm just curious that's all," replied Tilly, trying to keep her voice from trembling.

Sybil Heliot threw down her duster.

"It went to live with a man in Dorset who gives donkey rides. Now, if you don't mind," she bellowed, "I need to get on without any further interruption!" And with that, she turned and stomped off towards the kitchen.

Tilly steadied herself as she watched the intimidating figure sweep from the room. So, it appeared, they wouldn't find Willow on the East Coast beach after all. She knew Dorset was miles away. The family had had a caravan holiday there once. There was no way she could get there without help from the grown-ups. Inevitably, this news was going to make Sam even sadder.

CHAPTER 11

A Trip to Town

TWO WEEKS had flown by since the Millpeppers arrived at Dingleby Hall. Finally, their new home was straight, just in time for their first guests.

With great excitement, Dad and Tilly met Leila and her mother Ann off the 8.30 a.m. train from London. While Dad helped with their bags, Tilly and Leila chatted away. There was so much news for the girls to catch up on.

Arriving back at Dingleby Hall, Mum and Grammy were waiting eagerly at the front door to greet their visitors.

"Ann, welcome! I'm so glad you could make it," cried Mum, throwing her arms around her. She and Ann had been friends since their school days, so it had been a joyous time when their own daughters had become best friends as well.

"We're so excited to be here and to be getting out of London for a while," said Ann. "Lloyd sends his apologies, by the way. He's too busy at work at the moment to take any time off."

"I must admit Archie's disappointed. He was really looking forward to showing Lloyd his workshop. Never mind, another time."

"It looks a lovely place. You're so lucky."

"Let's not stand out here," said Mum. "Come in, there's so much I want to show you, and it's been ages since we've had a chance for a good natter. Tilly, why don't you show Leila up to your bedroom?"

Tearing up the staircase, Tilly led Leila into her room.

"Awesome, this is huge!" exclaimed Leila. "Am I sleeping in here with you?" she asked, noticing two made-up beds.

"Yes of course. Come on, I can't wait to introduce you to Sam."

✳ ✳ ✳

Sam was standing in his usual place in the paddock, swishing his tail against the pesky flies. However, the minute he heard Tilly's voice, his ears twitched and he trotted over to her. They had both agreed that for the time being it was best she didn't tell Leila that they could talk to each other. So, when Sam came to a standstill in front of them, he simply nudged Tilly, who in turn stroked his nose.

"He's a beauty, Tilly. Still, I'm really surprised you've learned to ride him. You never showed any interest in ponies when I started my lessons."

"I know, but having Sam has changed my mind. Did you bring your riding things?"

"Yes of course. I've been looking forward to riding in the countryside. The parks in London are OK," said Leila, looking around her, "but here there's so much open space."

"I told you Edie's mum owns a riding school, didn't I?" asked Tilly.

"Yes, several times."

"Only," continued Tilly, hardly pausing for breath, "she said she would loan you one of her ponies while you're here. We're going to keep it in the field with Sam."

"Oh, that's really nice of her."

"Yes, she's a lovely lady. Mum told her we couldn't collect it, though, until this evening, because she has to go into town to see a solicitor about Dingleby Hall. She insists we go with her, by the way, so you and your mum can look round the shops."

✳ ✳ ✳

At eleven o'clock, all the women bundled into the people carrier. Dad, who had already started working from home, was in his study with the door shut. Poppa and Bradley were both busy in the garden clearing out the greenhouse. Mum drove the car out of the drive and down the lane.

They were heading for Middlington, which was the closest town, about four miles from Little Abbot. It was quite a small town, but had a good variety of shops and places to eat. Mum made a beeline for the solicitors as soon as they arrived, while the rest of them were left to stroll around the High Street. Grammy and Ann were both interested in shopping for clothes, whilst Tilly and Leila wanted to find the equestrian shop recommended to them by Edie. So, the grown-ups decided to let the girls do their own thing, and later they would all meet up at one-thirty at the pizza restaurant for lunch.

The Horse Centre was some way from the High Street. It was full of everything you could want for the horse and rider. Tilly soon realised how lucky she was that the tack room back at the Hall seemed to already have most things she needed. But it was interesting looking around the place, nonetheless. Picking up a beginner's book on riding and pony care, she paid for it with the £5 Poppa had given her to treat herself before they left. Leila, on the other hand, hummed and hawed for a long time about buying a hoof pick. Eventually, she decided not to spend all her holiday money on the first day and settled, instead, for a yellow pencil with a rubber in the shape of a horse's head stuck on the end.

Walking back out into the street, they glanced at their phones and realised they hadn't much time left before they had to meet the grown-ups for lunch.

"We'd better get going," insisted Tilly. "Grammy will only start to worry if we're late."

They had only gone a few steps when Leila stopped at the entrance to a dark passageway.

"How about cutting through this alleyway, then?" suggested Leila. "Only, I think it'll be quicker."

"OK, I'll blame you if we get lost."

Striding along the narrow cobbled path, Tilly

came to an abrupt halt in front of an antique shop. Arranged on a table in the window display, a painting in a gold frame had caught her attention. If she wasn't mistaken, it was a painting of Dingleby Hall, just like the one she had seen in the old photo album Mum had found.

"Let's go in," insisted Tilly, grabbing Leila's arm. "I want to ask the shopkeeper where it came from."

The little bell over the door tinkled loudly as they entered. Stepping down into the dark interior, a stuffy, musty smell immediately hit their nostrils. The whole place was crammed full to bursting with piles of timeworn books, old clocks, numerous ornaments and even toys from children long ago. It was just like Aladdin's cave. Weaving their way carefully towards the counter, the girls immediately noticed an elderly gentleman perched on a high stool. He was reading from a tatty-looking book.

Without looking up from the faded pages, he grunted, "What can I do for you young ladies?"

"I'm interested in the painting in the window," stuttered Tilly. "Is it of Dingleby Hall?"

He looked over his rimless glasses, set his book down on the counter and stared at them.

"You know Dingleby Hall?" he asked.

"Yes, my family and I have just moved in there," pointed out Tilly.

"Interesting," he began, getting to his feet.

"You're correct. It is a wonderful painting of the Hall. Do you think your parents might want to buy it?" he asked enthusiastically, as his glasses fell to the end of his nose.

They might do," replied Tilly. "Can you tell me how it came to be in your shop?"

Straightening up, he immediately readjusted his glasses.

"I can tell you exactly how I got it, young lady! – not that it's any of your business. I found it lying in a ditch near Briary Woods a few months ago. It was just as well it hadn't rained; otherwise it would have been ruined. Naturally, being an honest man, I took it straight to the police station. The police made inquiries on my behalf, but it hadn't been reported stolen so eventually they told me I could keep it."

Tilly looked thoughtful.

"I'm sure my mum would like to see it. I'll bring her back here if we have time."

Returning to the alleyway the girls walked quickly towards the High Street.

"That was weird, don't you think?" remarked Leila.

"You're not kidding," replied Tilly. "I remember Uncle Leo telling me once to trust my first instinct, because more often than not it's right... You know, Leila, the more I think about it, the more I'm sure it was the painting from the Hall. But what I don't understand is how it ended up in a ditch near a wood!"

When the girls arrived at the pizza restaurant, the grown-ups were already sitting down at a table. Grammy, though, was outside anxiously pacing up and down the pavement.

"I tried to call you," cried Grammy, "but it went straight to voicemail. I was getting so worried, I thought something had happened to the two of you." She hugged both girls. "Come on, we've already ordered."

Mum was sitting with Ann and was in the middle of telling her about her meeting with the solicitor.

"He was only a young man. I asked him what had happened to the contents of the house, but he didn't seem to know. He said he would ask the senior partner of the firm, a Mr Hardcastle, when he returned from his around-the-world cruise. Apparently, he was the one who always dealt with my aunt's finances."

"Did you bring up the subject of Sybil Heliot?" asked Grammy.

"Yes, I did. Seemingly, she only started working for my aunt a month before she died. She has a contract of employment for six months, so we have to keep her for another six weeks."

"Pity," replied Grammy, biting hard into her pizza slice.

"Mum," broke in Tilly, "Leila and I saw a painting of Dingleby Hall in an antique shop. You must come and have a look at it. I think it's the one in the photo album…"

"Oh, Tilly dear, I'm sure there are many paintings of Dingleby Hall. It's quite famous around here. It's very unlikely the one you saw in the shop is the one my aunt owned. I'm guessing her painting is in the hands of some rich collector."

Tilly folded her arms and kicked the table leg. She was annoyed. All she wanted was her mum to have a look at the painting, because if she did, Tilly was sure she would say it was Great Aunt Phoebe's. She wasn't going to give up, though. Somehow she would prove the painting was the one from the Hall.

CHAPTER 12

Briary Woods

WHEN THEY got back from Middlington later that afternoon, Dad was excited about something he wanted to show Tilly.

"Tilly," he said quietly, "come and look at this. You're not going to believe it."

He pushed open the door to his study, and Tilly was astonished to see Dexter asleep in his basket with Jellicle curled up beside him, one of her front paws stretched out as if she were cuddling her new doggy friend. Tilly was delighted that it looked like Dexter and Jellicle had actually become friends at last.

Just after six, with Sam saddled and bridled, Tilly and Leila set off for the Little Abbot Riding School, only a short walk away.

Edie was waiting for them at the gate, which was the entrance to the yard, when they arrived. The yard was a large concreted area, encircled by numerous stables. The heads of several inquisitive horses of all sizes and colours peered out from the tops of their stable doors. Some were munching hay between their enormous teeth. Others simply whinnied and threw their heads in the air, seemingly greeting Sam as his hooves clip-clopped over the hard surface. All of a sudden, one of the stable doors opened and Jo emerged leading a pony.

"You made it, then. I was almost giving up," said Jo. "Hi, you must be Leila. It's nice to meet you. Tilly tells me you've been riding for a while."

"Since I was four," replied Leila proudly.

"Excellent. This is Star. I'm sure you'll find her an easy ride."

Leila stepped forward, stretched out her arm and stroked the pony's nose. Star was a chestnut filly, about the same size as Sam. She had four white socks and, tucked behind her forelock, a small area of white hair that had grown into the shape of a five-pointed star.

"She's beautiful," said Leila. "Thank you for letting me ride her while I'm here."

"You're welcome," replied Jo. "She's actually Felix's pony. But he and his family are away on holiday at the moment, so they asked me to find someone to ride her. By the way, I'm hoping both you and Tilly will take part in our show this weekend. Edie said she's already mentioned it to you, Tilly?"

"You will, won't you?" cried Edie.

"I'm game," enthused Leila. "What about you Tilly?"

Tilly hesitated. "I don't feel ready yet for competitions. I've only just started riding. But Sam and I will come along anyway."

"Great," said Jo. "OK, let's see you mount, Leila. Then I suggest we all go for a short hack along the lanes, before we ride on to the Hall."

Back at Sam's field, a couple of hours later, with the sun dipping below the horizon, Tilly and Leila watched their two ponies getting to know each other.

"It's nice to see Sam with a friend," said Tilly. "He's been so sad since Willow left."

"You can read his mind then, can you?" grinned Leila.

"In a way," replied Tilly, stopping herself from telling her best friend her secret.

* * *

The girls got up early the following day, excited for their morning ride. At breakfast Leila brought up the subject of the Pony Club show.

"It's the first I've heard of it," exclaimed Mum. "Tilly, do you want to join the Pony Club?"

Tilly stirred her spoon around in her cereal bowl.

"I wouldn't mind," replied Tilly. "Edie did say it was great fun."

"Well, that settles it," said Dad. "I'll pay for you to join."

Before Tilly could say anything more, Leila piped up, "Mum, Jo said I could take part in the Pony Club show, even if I'm not a member. I would love to go in a jumping competition, but Star and I have nowhere to practise."

"I thought there were jumps in the training area," pointed out Grammy.

"There are, Grammy," said Tilly, "but most of them are damaged or completely broken."

"Leave it to me," cried Dad, with a big smile crossing his face at the thought of putting his carpentry skills to good use. "I'll build you the best set of jumps in the village."

Tilly stood up and gave her dad a big hug.

"Thanks, Dad, for the Pony Club membership and for volunteering to make the jumps. You're the best dad in the whole world." Dad beamed. "Come on Leila," Tilly continued, "we'd better get the ponies ready. Edie said she'd be here at ten."

Arriving at the field, Tilly was surprised not to find Sam standing in his usual place. Instead he was busy grazing alongside Star. However, his ears soon pricked up on hearing the girls' voices. Raising his head, he immediately trotted over to them.

"You've got him well trained, Tilly," said Leila.

"Nothing to do with me. He's trained himself," replied Tilly, flinging her arms around her pony's neck. "Why don't you see if you can catch Star? She's wearing a halter, so you shouldn't have too much trouble."

Tilly watched Leila striding across the paddock, before turning and whispering to Sam, "Have you ever been to Briary Wood?"

Sam pulled a face. "I've ridden past it several times. These days it's a creepy place. We animals try to avoid it if we can."

"Creepy?"

Sam pulled another face. "It's said, if you go in, you're never seen again."

Tilly's eyes widened, then she shook her head in disbelief. "I'm sure that must be just a silly tale to keep people out. Come on, I can see Leila's caught Star. I'd better get you ready for the ride."

Just after ten, Edie arrived on her pony, Peter, and the three friends made their way out of the Hall's grounds, towards the nearest bridle path. Keen to see if she could find any clues as to why the painting of Dingleby Hall ended up in a ditch, Tilly asked Edie if they could ride to Briary Woods.

"OK, I'll take you," said Edie, "on the understanding we don't actually go in. I'm never going in there again!"

"Why?" piped up Leila.

Tears rose in Edie's eyes. "A few months ago, Yee Zhu, a boy in our class, was out walking with his parents when their dog suddenly ran off into the woods. Yee followed him… Neither of them have been seen since." She wiped a tear from her cheek.

Wow, that's such a sad story," said Leila.

"His poor parents, how awful," added Tilly.

"They searched for him for weeks without any sign," continued Edie. "Since then, no one from the village has dared to enter, and there's police notices everywhere saying '*Keep Out*'. Anyway, the wood is so thick with trees now, there isn't a path to follow, even if you tried to go in."

"Look, don't worry. I don't actually want to go into the woods," explained Tilly. "I just want to have a look around the area. You never know we might find a clue as to why the painting ended up there."

After half an hour of riding along the marked bridleway, Edie veered her pony to the right. Approaching the dense woods, leaving the comfort of the bridle path far behind, the three young riders were all too soon aware of a stillness in the air. Even the once blue cloudless sky was growing noticeably darker, and the birds seemed to have stopped their singing. Briary Woods was certainly living up to its spooky reputation.

As they rode in silence alongside the wood, which seemed to stretch on forever, Tilly kept her eyes firmly to the ground. Suddenly she pulled on Sam's reins and leapt out of the saddle. There in the middle of a ditch, where she imagined the painting had been found, lay a small object half submerged in the mud. Reaching down, she drew it out of the sticky brown soil and studied it.

"What is it?" asked Leila.

"It's an ornament of some sort. I'll take it home and clean it up," said Tilly. Wrapping it in a tissue, she placed it in her backpack.

"Can we go home now?" pleaded Edie, looking around herself nervously. "I really don't like this place."

"OK, I must say I'm feeling a bit spooked too," admitted Tilly, quickly mounting Sam again. "Right, race you both back to the path."

*** * ***

Later, at Sam's paddock, Tilly and Leila watched with delight as their ponies cantered around the field together before settling down to feed on the grass. Removing the dirt-encrusted ornament from her backpack, Tilly walked over to the water tap by the pony's drinking trough. Holding it under the running water, she cleaned it thoroughly before lifting it up to the light. It was a china figure of a Victorian lady. She was dressed all in

blue, apart from her white bonnet.

"Do you think it's got something to do with the painting?" asked Leila, as the two girls stood gazing at it.

"I don't know," replied Tilly, examining it more closely.

Turning it over, Tilly's eyes focused immediately on a rubber stopper wedged into the base. She tried her best to pull it out, but her wet fingers couldn't budge it. She passed it over to Leila, and was pleased to see her friend having more luck. The stopper was beginning to loosen.

"Well done!" exclaimed Tilly, as Leila stood triumphant with the stopper in one hand and the ornament in the other.

"There seems to be something inside," cried Leila, peering into the hole the stopper had left. Carefully she eased out a roll of yellowing paper and unravelled it. "What do you think it is? Some ancient recipe?" she wondered, squinting her eyes trying to read it. Giving up, she handed it to Tilly.

"That's exactly what it looks like," said Tilly, studying the aged sheet in front of her. "The words are impossible to read, though. I'm guessing it's in old English. I wonder why it was hidden in there. We'll probably never know. Oh well, we'd better put it back for now." She sighed. "I wish Uncle Leo was here. He loves mysteries like this. He'd solve it in no time."

Making their way back to the house, with the ornament safely in Tilly's backpack, they both agreed not to mention their find to anyone else for the time being.

CHAPTER 13

Picklewick-on-Sea

LUNCH WAS already on the table when the girls appeared in the kitchen. Naturally, the grown-ups were keen to hear how their ride had gone. Neither Tilly nor Leila mentioned finding the china ornament or visiting Briary Woods, just in case Tilly's Mum had heard the story of Yee Zhu. Tilly didn't want to worry her unduly.

When lunch was finished, Grammy suggested going to the seaside since it was such a lovely day. Excited by the prospect, all three children ran upstairs to get their swimming things.

As they descended the staircase, with their costumes wrapped in their towels, the front door opened. Sybil Heliot had arrived a little early. Leila stopped halfway down the stairs and stared at her. She couldn't help it. Tilly had talked so much about Sybil Heliot. Why was she so surprised at finally meeting her? Tilly was right. She did look like a witch. Completely ignoring the children, Sybil Heliot took herself into the sitting room and closed the door firmly behind her.

Picklewick-on-Sea was a typical English seaside town. It had a long promenade with a low wall and railings. Steep steps led down to a crowded sandy beach. On the opposite side of the road, a line of shops sold all sorts of things, including buckets and spades, in fact everything you'd need to enjoy your time at the beach. There were numerous cafés selling fish and chips and several noisy arcades, which Bradley headed to as soon as he got out of the car. Whilst Grammy and Poppa kept an eye on Bradley, Mum and Ann walked down to the beach with Tilly and Leila.

They hired loungers and positioned themselves in the shade under an enormous beige umbrella. Changing quickly into their costumes, the girls screamed with delight as they ran into the sea. The salty water was cold (so very cold) but, with the intense heat of the summer's day, refreshing at the same time. Wading in up to their waists, they swam for ages amongst the waves, jumping at the biggest ones, which roared with great force towards the shore. Beginning to turn a shade of blue, they both decided they needed to warm up and ran back up the beach to get their towels. Mum asked them if they would like an ice cream, to which they replied *yes please* and, without hesitation, set off for the ice cream van parked on the beach.

There was already a long queue of people. Everyone it seemed wanted an ice cream or a lolly. Bored with having to wait, Tilly looked around her. That's when she caught sight of the man giving donkey rides. She nudged Leila.

"Let's get our ice creams and take a closer look."

After handing their mums their ice cream cones (each with a chocolate flake), the two friends set off across the beach. There were six donkeys, of differing sizes, waiting for riders. They were all standing quietly in a row, tied securely by their reins to a long thick rope. Their names were clearly printed on their browbands.

Tilly sighed, "I suppose this is what Willow's doing down in Dorset. I feel quite sorry for the poor things."

"They don't look too unhappy," said Leila. "I've heard stories of how badly donkeys are treated in some other parts of the world that would make you cry."

"I suppose you're right. Hopefully they have a field to run around in after working here," suggested Tilly, imagining the donkeys kicking up their heels in a green meadow full of yellow buttercups.

It seemed a man with a hunched back and a large money belt around his waist was in charge. The minute Tilly and Leila got nearer he asked them if they wanted a ride.

"Its £2.50," he growled, jingling his money belt at them, "cheap for this beach."

"I'm sure it is," replied Tilly. "I'll have to ask my mum. I haven't any money on me. Can we stroke them?"

The man sniffed. "Yeah, go on. Careful though, some of the blighters bite."

If some of them bite, thought Tilly, then they shouldn't be giving rides to kids, surely. They went over to the tethered donkeys and rubbed their heads. They seemed docile enough. It was then they noticed three more donkeys approaching at a fast trot. Their young riders were bouncing on their backs, bare arms and legs flapping in the air as they shouted, "Giddy up horsey!"

A woman in stripy shorts stepped forward. Seemingly, she was the children's mother.

"Did you enjoy that?" she asked them.

The oldest of the three, a boy whose head had been recently shaved, cried, "They were too slow. I wanted to go faster! Can I have another go on that one?" He pointed to the largest donkey, called Adam.

"Not today," replied his mother, her cheeks flushing a very bright red.

"But we want another go!" all three of her brood screamed.

"Not today!" she repeated, before dragging her ungrateful children away.

"Are you gonna have a ride or not?" asked the man, addressing Tilly impatiently. "Only I'm packin' up soon."

Tilly moved closer to the donkeys the three children had been riding. Reaching towards the smallest one, she rubbed the little donkey's head. Across the red browband, in bold letters it read 'WILLOW'. Was it just a coincidence? She supposed Willow wasn't an unusual name for a donkey.

"Yes, I'd like a ride," replied Tilly. "I'll just run and get some money. Can I ride this one?"

"If you're bloomin' quick. I can't promise, you know. She's popular is our Willow."

Sprinting back along the beach, kicking up sand as they ran, Leila suddenly stopped to catch her breath. "Tilly, you're not thinking it's the donkey from the Hall, are you?"

"No, but just in case I want you to take a

picture of me riding her."

"Surely you're not going to show it to Sybil Heliot?"

"No, I've got someone else in mind."

The minute they reached home, Tilly dashed up to Sam's field before Leila realised she'd gone. Sam was standing with Star under the large tree. She called his name, and he came cantering over to her.

"I've got something to show you," she said, and took out her phone. "Is this Willow?"

Sam looked long and hard at the picture, then shook his head.

"No, it's not."

Tilly bowed her head, her eyes misted over.

"I'm sorry. I thought it might be," she said, reaching up and stroking his ear. "I will find her one day, Sam. I promise."

CHAPTER 14

The Pony Club Show

LEILA WAS feeling sad. It was only two days before the show and she and Star had hardly been able to practise their jumping. Between them, the girls had managed to cobble a couple of jumps together out of fallen branches and a few bricks, but they were hardly anywhere near professional. Leila didn't feel she could press Tilly's dad about the jumps he had promised. After all, she was a guest in their house, and she knew he was busy most of the time working in his study.

At breakfast, Dad announced he had to go into London for a meeting. Leila looked down at her half-eaten toast and sighed. Then Dad grinned before telling them there was a surprise waiting for them in the arena. Excusing themselves from the table, the girls ran eagerly towards the stables. There, in the practice ring, four beautifully-painted jumps had been erected. Attached to a white post was a note from Dad. It said he was sorry he hadn't managed to finish all of them yet before the horse show, but he hoped these would do for the time being.

"Poppa and I helped Dad put the finishing touches to them late last night," announced Bradley proudly, as he and an over-excited Dexter joined them. "I even helped with the painting. What do you think, Short Stuff, good or what?"

"They're brilliant," replied Tilly.

"They sure are," enthused Leila.

"I can't wait until Sam and I are ready to try them," added Tilly.

"I'm going to get Star and have a go right now!"

Leila spent almost an hour putting her pony

over the jumps until a bored Star, deciding she'd had enough, stopped suddenly in front of a double jump made up of two green and white poles. At this point, Leila lost her balance and slid unceremoniously out of the saddle.

"I think Star's had enough, Leila," said Tilly, running to help her friend now sprawled on the ground. "Shall we go for a ride? It looks like it's going to rain soon."

They spent the rest of the morning riding along the lanes, trying to dodge the frequent showers. Although they all ended up drenched, the ponies seemed to enjoy the outing.

✳ ✳ ✳

It was the day of the horse show. The girls were up early giving their mounts a thorough grooming. They even washed their manes and tails. At last, both ponies had been cleaned to perfection. Now they had to get tidied up themselves. Leaving the ponies in the stables so they didn't have the chance to roll in the dirt, the girls ran inside to get changed.

The dress code for the Pony Club, of which Tilly was now a member, was very specific. It consisted of a white shirt with the Pony Club tie and beige jodhpurs. As Tilly only had blue jodhpurs, Leila had to lend her a pair of hers. Back at the stables, both ponies were waiting with their heads over the doors. Once tacked up with their freshly cleaned saddles and bridles, they were all finally ready. The grown-ups, full of enthusiasm for their daughters, appeared for a last-minute inspection.

"You both look great, very neat and tidy," exclaimed Ann.

"Let's hope the rain keeps off," said Poppa, looking up at the sky.

"I'm very proud of you both," said Mum. "Now off you go and good luck. We'll follow you down."

✳ ✳ ✳

Little Abbot's Riding School was bustling with numerous horseboxes and cars. There were lots of spectators already milling around or sitting on the chairs surrounding the enormous show ring, which was situated in a corner of a twenty-acre field. It was all very exciting.

Tilly's family soon arrived with Ann and managed to find themselves seats around the show ring. They hadn't been there long when a voice boomed out from a loudspeaker with a final call to all competitors to register in The Green Tent.

"Go on, that's you," cried Tilly.

"And you," returned Leila. "Aren't you going in for best turned out?"

"I don't know now. Look at all the beautiful horses. I really don't think I can."

"Nonsense. If I can go in for the junior jumping competition, you can at least enter the best turned out. You only have to walk in a circle. Come on, let's tie the ponies up over there under

125

the trees with the others. We don't want them getting hot and bothered."

They dismounted and led their ponies in the direction of the resting area. Soon after they had registered in The Green Tent, they caught sight of Edie on Peter.

"I'm so glad you both came. What have you entered?" asked Edie.

"I'm going in the under-twelves' jumping and Tilly is in the under-twelves' best turned out," replied Leila, as she attached the number 52 to her shirt, before helping Tilly with her number, 49.

"Excellent. Peter and I have entered the bending race and the jumping. May the best rider and pony win!" grinned Edie. "If you want refreshments, The Big Barn is full of stalls selling food and drink. By the way, you won't see much of my mum during the day. She's a quivering wreck as always, running here and there... Have you seen Bella yet?"

"She's here then?" answered Tilly.

"Yes, she and Ms Heliot arrived a while ago. As I said before, you can't miss her… Wasn't that the call for your event, Tilly?"

"Oh no!" cried Tilly, the colour draining from her face.

"Come on, Leila and I will go with you. You'll be fine," assured Edie.

Collecting Sam from beneath the trees, Tilly scrambled into the saddle. Leaning forward, she whispered, "Let's show them, Sam."

Sam snorted and arched his neck. His black, clean, shiny tail fanned out in the gentle breeze. He knew exactly what was expected of him. There seemed to be quite a few riders in their event – Tilly counted at least twelve. As they entered the show ring, a man in a Panama hat (who Tilly presumed was the judge) told them to follow the pony in front. She and Sam rode behind a little girl on a white Shetland pony, who seemed to be more interested in the grass than riding in a circle. The hungry pony kept going out of line and the poor girl had a job to haul her back each time. In the end she gave up and burst into tears. A woman ran into the show ring and led the sobbing girl and her pony away.

Eventually, the judge told the group to halt. Then he inspected each pony and rider in turn.

"Will the following numbers please step forward," instructed the Judge, "105, 86, 17 and 49."

Tilly looked dazed. A cry went up from the crowd. It was Grammy.

"Tilly! You're number 49!"

Pulling herself together, Tilly clicked and Sam moved forward. What was the judge saying? Did he say dismount? She gazed around her. It appeared she was the only one left in the line still sitting on their pony, so she dismounted quickly. Holding onto the reins, she stood nervously beside Sam.

"Please would you all remove your saddles?" commanded the judge.

Tilly was thankful she had given Sam a thorough grooming. Then, before she really understood what was happening, she was being handed a red rosette and the spectators were clapping loudly. Riding Sam out of the ring, she was greeted by her family.

"Well done!" exclaimed everyone.

Tilly beamed from ear to ear. She'd won a first place, but to be honest, she was just relieved it was all over.

"You did it," cried Edie, patting Sam's neck as they walked back over to the trees. "Oh, oh, don't look now, but Ms Heliot is walking towards us alongside Bella on Orion."

Striding in their direction, Sybil Heliot's mouth seemed to be making an effort to smile, but was failing miserably.

I see you got a first," she began haughtily. "I'm hoping Bella will do just as well in the jumping."

Bella Heliot, whose eyes were even greener and her hair blacker than her mother's, was sitting stiffly in the saddle. As she held tightly onto the reins, her knuckles were turning noticeably white.

Before she could stop herself (regretting her words the minute they left her lips), Tilly said, "She's got strong competition. Both Leila and Edie have entered the jumping as well."

Sybil Heliot's nose rose once again. "We shall see," she replied snootily. "Come Bella, I could do with a drink." She looked closer at her daughter.

"You have dirt on the back of your hand. Clean it off immediately!"

Without a word, Bella raised her hand to her mouth and licked the back of it, a look of satisfaction in her eyes. Then she gave Orion a sudden kick in his side, and the pony took off at full pelt with Sybil Heliot running on behind. Tilly watched quizzically as the trio went out of view. There had been something about Bella's behaviour that was familiar to Tilly. She couldn't put a finger on it right now, but she reminded her of someone.

"So that was Bella," blurted out Tilly. "Anyone else notice that she didn't say a word?"

"Come to think of it, she never says much," returned Edie.

"Well, her pony's going to be exhausted before the jumping begins if she carries on like she is," pointed out Tilly. "Come on, let's get back to the show ring. I want to watch the other competitions."

Before they knew it, it was lunchtime – time for a break while the show ring was made ready for the jumping. With the ponies keeping cool under the trees, Tilly, Leila and Edie went off to The Big Barn for something to eat and drink. They all decided on hot dogs and chips, plus bottles of water, and then went back outside to find a nice shady spot to sit down to eat.

"I have to say I'm enjoying my first horse show," enthused Tilly, before taking a big bite out of her hot dog.

"I'm glad," replied Edie. "Next time, I'm sure you'll be able to enter more events."

Leila shaded her eyes.

"Tilly, look over there. Isn't that the man and his donkeys from the seaside?"

"Oh, you've met Old Man Spencer, then?" mused Edie. "He brings his donkeys here every year."

"Leila and I met him a few days ago," replied Tilly, looking over to where Leila was pointing.

"He has a donkey called Willow. I thought there was a chance it was the one from the Hall, but it turns out it's not." She stood up. "I'm going over to have another word with him."

Before she could do so, though, she noticed Sybil Heliot making her way in the man's direction. Frantically waving her arms about, Sybil Heliot was leaning right up into Old Man Spencer's face. From where Tilly was standing, it looked like she was telling him off. She really wished she could hear what they were talking about.

The call for competitors for the junior jumping echoed around the field. Leila and Edie leapt to their feet and started to make their way towards their ponies. The minute Leila saw the jumps, her face drained of colour.

"I don't think I'm ready," she announced.

"Nonsense, you'll be fine. Star knows what she's doing. She's jumped those jumps before. After all, this is her home," pointed out Edie.

"Are you coming with us Tilly?"

"I'll be over in a minute. Don't worry, I won't miss seeing you jump. I just want to have a word with Old Man Spencer."

"Tilly," whispered Leila quietly, "I thought you said it wasn't Willow? Anyway," she continued, "you never did tell me who you showed the picture to?"

Tilly looked down at her feet and kicked the ground. "I showed it to Sam. He told me it wasn't her."

Leila's eyes almost popped out of her head, and then she threw her head back and laughed.

"No, honestly, who did you ask?"

"I told you. It was Sam," insisted Tilly. Now looking directly into Leila's eyes, she placed her hand on her friend's shoulder. "It's a long story. I'll explain later. Go on, get ready. They'll be calling you soon."

The smile dropped from Leila's face. What did Tilly mean? She didn't want to leave her. She wanted to ask her more questions. Reluctantly, she turned away and caught up with Edie, while Tilly made her way towards the donkeys. Fortunately, Sybil Heliot was no longer in sight.

"Hello," said Tilly.

"It's £3 a ride," growled Old Man Spencer, without looking at her.

"I don't want a ride," replied Tilly, realising Old Man Spencer had raised his prices. "I had one on the beach the other day, remember? I just wanted to say hi to the donkeys." Old Man Spencer was irritated. He was there to make money. This silly girl was wasting his time. "Where's Willow, by the way?" added Tilly, paying no attention at all to the man's obvious annoyance. "Only, she doesn't appear to be here."

"Willow? Yeah, she is. She's the one on the end."

Tilly looked towards the donkey with 'WILLOW' printed on its browband.

"That's not the same donkey called Willow you

had the other day!"

Exasperated by Tilly's continuous questions, he grunted, "I don't always put the same bridles on the same bloomin' donkeys! Today that's bloomin' Willow! Now let me get on!"

Tilly stood staring at the animals. Was it possible? Could one of these donkeys actually be the real Willow? Sybil Heliot obviously knew Old Man Spencer. Was he the man who took Sam's friend away?

CHAPTER 15

A Secret Revealed

BEFORE TILLY had time to think any more about Willow, a voice came over the loudspeaker calling for all competitors in the junior jumping competition. As she had promised to be back, she had no choice but to leave the donkeys for now and re-join her friends.

Half an hour later, the competition was well underway. So far, no one had managed a clear round. The closest anyone had come was a farmer's boy on a large, strawberry roan cob, but unfortunately for him the pony refused at the final jump. Attempting to jump it again, his pony had taken off too early and struck the poles on the way up, unseating the farmer's boy in mid-air.

The next competitor was a girl called Primrose,

on a bay pony. They didn't get any further than the first jump, which was made of brushwood with a blue and yellow pole on top. Her pony had stopped in front of it, extended its neck and to the girl's total embarrassment, started pulling out the brushwood. In fact, in its eagerness to dine on the dry twigs, her pony completely demolished the jump. As a result, Primrose was asked to leave the ring in order for the wrecked jump to be rebuilt. This all took several long minutes.

Leila was a complete bag of nerves when her number was eventually called. With *'Good luck, Leila'* ringing in her ears, she rode Star to the first jump, and as good as her name, the little pony popped over it with no trouble at all. Completing the course with just four faults, Leila's face beamed as they left the ring.

"Well done, darling!" cried Ann. "I'm just sorry your dad wasn't here to see you."

In the middle of congratulating her friend, Tilly cried, "Look everyone, it's Ms Heliot's daughter Bella up next!"

Rushing back to the ringside to get a better view, Tilly noticed Bella was still sitting stiffly in the saddle as she and Orion entered the ring. The poor pony already looked hot and bothered – white, foaming lather was dripping down his satin black neck. Holding him on too tight a rein, Bella launched him at the first jump at such speed that they almost crashed into the second one. Then it happened. Coming to the end of a series of jumps,

Bella turned him to the right instead of the left. A cry of '*You're going the wrong way!*' went up from the crowd, but it was too late. They were eliminated – much to the utter disgust of Sybil Heliot.

Following Bella, there were only three more competitors. Edie rode Peter into the ring, and immediately you could tell the little pony was going to enjoy himself. They managed a superb clear round as did the last entrant, a boy on a dapple-grey pony. As a consequence, they had to have a jump off between them over a higher and shorter course. The boy did another clear round and whooped loudly at the end of it, frightening his pony so much it bolted out of the ring. Somehow or other, though, he managed to hang on. Sadly, Peter clipped a jump with his near hind hoof to finish with four faults. This meant that the boy was first, Edie was second, and a delighted Leila was third. As Leila collected her yellow rosette, Ann was almost exploding with pride.

With her friends' competitions completed,

Tilly's thoughts turned back to the donkeys. Leaving everyone watching the next jumping event, she went over to Sam and untied him.

"Sam, there's someone I want you to meet."

Leading him towards the area where the donkeys had been giving rides, she found to her dismay there was no longer any sign of them. Seeing Jo talking to somebody's parent, she ran over to her.

"Are you enjoying yourself, Tilly?" Jo asked.

"Yeah, we're all having a great time… Have you any idea where the donkeys have gone?"

Jo took a big intake of breath. "Good question. Mr Spencer suddenly told me he had double booked, which is really annoying. He left about half an hour ago."

Oh no, thought Tilly, patting Sam's neck. She had been hoping he could identify Old Man Spencer as the man who took Willow away. Obviously, that wasn't going to happen now.

✸ ✸ ✸

It had been a long but exciting day. With the ponies back in their paddock all fed and watered, Leila and Tilly were up in Tilly's bedroom relaxing and listening to music.

"Tilly," began Leila, "you said something funny at the horse show. Do you remember? You said you could talk to Sam. It was a joke, right?"

Tilly got up from her bed and walked over to her chest of drawers. Reaching into the back of the top drawer, she pulled out the Wishing Stone.

"Uncle Leo gave this to me on my birthday," she said, handing Leila the smooth, yellow stone. "He told me it was a wishing stone."

"OK…" replied Leila hesitantly, turning the stone over in her hand to reveal the tiger with the large paws.

"I made a wish to be able to talk to animals," continued Tilly. "At first nothing happened and then I found the only animal I could talk to was Sam. But I think that's because the Wishing Stone wanted me to find out why he was so sad, so I could help him. I think it's a very clever wishing stone."

Leila gawped open-mouthed at her friend.

"OK…" she repeated slowly. "I'm not saying I don't believe you, but…"

"Come on, then," cried Tilly, eagerly putting her boots back on her feet. "Let me show you."

Marching towards Sam's field, Tilly called him, and he came cantering over.

"Sam, I've told Leila you and I can talk to each other. How can we prove it to her?"

"How about you give me some instructions?" suggested Sam.

"OK, I can see his lips moving," revealed Leila, focusing on Sam's mouth, "but no words are coming out."

"I suppose, because the Wishing Stone granted me the wish, I'm the only one who can hear him," suggested Tilly. "Sam said I should give him an instruction, so here goes. Sam, can I have a lift to the top of the field, please?"

To Leila's astonishment, Sam immediately got down on his front knees and Tilly clambered on. Trotting to the top of the field, he stopped and Tilly jumped off. She then asked him to go back for Leila. Tilly smiled as she watched Leila climbing onto Sam's back, before making their way towards her.

"Now Sam, can you walk clockwise around the field. Leila, hold on!"

Several more instructions later and Leila was convinced.

"Wow, this is amazing!" cried Leila. "What a wonderful gift!"

"I know," beamed Tilly, as Leila slid off Sam's back. "I feel very lucky. Do you understand now why I have to find Willow?"

"Yes, of course, and I'll help you."

* * *

The following morning, the girls set off for a ride along the lanes. It had rained heavily in the night and the ground was soft and the air had that fresh and clean smell about it. Unintentionally, they found themselves heading for Briary Wood. Whilst they were on the bridle path, Sam suddenly stopped and pawed at the ground.

"There's a rider up ahead," he announced.

"What's the matter with Sam?" asked Leila.

"He says there's a rider up ahead… Is it someone we know, Sam?"

"It's the monster's daughter."

Realising Sam meant Bella, she twisted round in the saddle to look at Leila.

"Apparently, it's Bella on Orion. Do you want to turn back?"

"I don't know why we should. We've as much right to ride these bridle paths as anyone else."

Walking on further, Tilly could feel the tension building in Sam's shoulders. She leaned forward to stroke his neck, to reassure him that everything was going to be fine. Leaving the safety of the path, they suddenly caught sight of Bella up ahead.

Clicking their ponies to a trot, so they could follow more closely, the girls were astonished to witness Bella and Orion disappearing from their sight, into the forbidden Briary Woods!

CHAPTER 16

An Enchanted Place

THE GIRLS sat staring in the direction they last saw Bella.

"She can't have disappeared already!" cried Tilly. "We can't just stand by and do nothing. Let's head over there and call her name. We have to warn her! She might not have heard about Yee Zhu or seen the police notices."

"Come on, then!"

With their ponies now at a canter, they arrived swiftly at the place Bella and Orion had vanished, and leapt from their saddles.

"I thought Edie said there wasn't a path into the woods," burst out Leila, peering through the gap between the trees. "There certainly seems to be one now... Bella!"

"Bella!" shrieked Tilly. "It's Tilly Millpepper from Dingleby Hall! I need to speak to you! Please come out of the woods! It's not safe!"

Minutes later, there was still no sign or sound of either Bella or Orion.

"I'm going to climb to the top of that tree," insisted Tilly, pointing towards a tall sycamore, "to see if I can see them."

"Do be careful, Tilly," cried Leila, watching anxiously as her friend sprinted towards the trunk of the old gnarled tree.

It didn't take Tilly long to reach the branches, giving her a bird's-eye view out over the woods.

"Can you see anything?" called Leila.

"I can see that the path goes on for quite a way, but there's no sign of Bella. I'll come down."

Re-joining Leila on the ground, Tilly had already decided what she had to do next.

"I'm going to follow the path. I'll leave Sam out here with you, because I know I'll never persuade him to go in. If I'm not back in twenty minutes, ride home and get help."

Leila shook her head.

"There's no way I'm letting you go in there on your own," she insisted. "It could be dangerous. We'll tie the ponies to a tree. They should be OK as long as we're not too long."

To be honest, Tilly was relieved Leila was going with her. Making their way along the winding track, they moved deeper and deeper into the unknown. The only sound they could hear was the crunching beneath their boots of the leaf-covered ground. There was no rustling of rabbits scampering for cover, or the call of birds from one to another. They seemed to be walking forever, until unexpectedly they came to a clearing. Even more unexpectedly, in the middle of the clearing was a crooked wooden house, with a crooked grey pillar of smoke coming from its single crooked chimney. There was still no sign of Bella or Orion.

Interested to know whose house it was, they

decided not to go on any further into the woods for the moment. Crouching down behind a large bush, they watched and waited.

And then...

"What are you two doing?" growled a gruff voice behind them that made them both jump.

"Bradders!" cried Tilly, spinning round. "You scared us! Why are you here?"

"I could ask you the same question, Short

Stuff," grinned Bradley. "I was taking Dexter for a walk and saw your ponies tied to a tree. I guessed you must have come in here. You shouldn't just leave them, you know. Anyone could ride off with them." He looked towards the house. "That's a funny looking place. I wonder who lives there?"

"We were wondering the same thing," replied Tilly. "Didn't you see the police notices? This wood is out of bounds. A boy disappeared in here a little while ago."

"Really, well, that's another reason you and Leila shouldn't have wandered in, then. Come on let's go back," he urged, grabbing his sister's arm.

Tilly pulled her arm away and stood her ground.

"No, we can't. We followed Ms Heliot's daughter in here. We think something awful must have happened to her, because there's no sign of her or her pony."

"I bet she rode straight through and is already on her way home. Come on," he pleaded, "Mum won't be too happy if I leave you here."

At that precise moment, the door of the wooden house creaked open and who should step out? None other than Sybil Heliot surrounded by several cats. The children gasped and instantly dropped to their knees. Even Dexter, who had been trying to sniff out furry creatures, stood motionless.

The three of them watched fearfully from their hiding place as Sybil Heliot looked around her. Mumbling something they were too far away to hear, she eventually turned and, to the children's relief, went back into the house. Her adoring cats following close at her heels.

"Wow!" said Bradley at last. "So, this is where the old biddy lives." Removing his phone from his pocket he took several pictures of the house and the surroundings.

"That means Bella lives here too," added Tilly, "but there's no sign of her or Orion."

"Come on, I think we should go," pleaded Leila. "I mean, we know now all Bella was doing was coming home."

"Don't you think it's odd, though," pondered Tilly, "that Edie told us the story of Yee Zhu, but didn't mention that Ms Heliot and Bella lived in the woods?"

"Perhaps she didn't know," pointed out Leila, "or perhaps Ms Heliot wasn't living here at the time. Come on let's go, this place is creeping me out… Tilly! Tilly! What are you doing?"

Tilly had begun to snake her way towards the house. On hearing the cries from her brother and her friend, she turned and put her finger to her lips for them not to make another sound. Keeping low to the ground, she reached the small window next to the front door. On an overturned metal bucket, she stood on tiptoe and squinted through the misty glass.

Inside, she could see that Sybil Heliot was standing in front of a huge black cauldron, which hung from a metal pole over a burning fire. Hovering beside her was a broomstick! The cats –

Tilly counted at least nine – were all focused on their mistress. As Tilly's eyes moved uneasily about the room, they finally came to rest on the far corner. Positioned on a three-legged stool was a tall, black, pointy hat... There was no doubt now. Sybil Heliot was a real broom-flying, wand-waving, cackling... witch!

Then the unfortunate happened. Tilly's foot slipped from the bucket, which made a loud clanking sound. Wobbling slightly, she tried her best to keep her balance, but in doing so made even more noise. Sybil Heliot's eyes were ablaze as her head turned towards the window. A great roar erupted from within the house and suddenly the angry face of Sybil Heliot was looking directly at Tilly.

"What are you doing here, Tilly Millpepper?" she hissed.

Tilly climbed down from the bucket and stared up at her.

"Um, we were looking for Bella. We thought

she might like to join us on our ride."

"We? Whose we?" Sybil Heliot screamed.

Recognising Sybil Heliot's high-pitched voice, Dexter suddenly made a run for it and kept on running right out of the woods.

Unaware of the scene Tilly had witnessed inside the house, Leila and Bradley watched with horror at the sight of Sybil Heliot towering over her. Leaving their hiding place, Leila and Bradley raced towards the house. Standing defiantly by Tilly's side, Leila took her friend's hand.

"We didn't mean any harm," insisted Leila, shaking slightly, "honestly."

"Well, well, what am I to do with the three of you?" snarled Sybil Heliot, placing her hands on her hips.

"You don't have to do anything with us," piped up Bradley bravely. "We'll just go. Come on girls!"

Sybil Heliot's arm stretched out and grabbed Bradley's shoulder, preventing him from moving a single step.

"Oh no," she sneered, "I can't let you go. You see you can see the path into the woods and my little house, when others can't. My powers must be fading fast." She stared directly at Tilly. "It's your family's fault. I didn't have enough time to find it!"

"Find what?" asked Tilly innocently.

Sybil Heliot shook her head.

"It's a long story. Why don't you come in, children, and I'll tell you all about it."

CHAPTER 17

A Witch's Tale

NOW IF a witch asked you into her house, what would you do? Run away? Yes, of course that would be the sensible thing to do. Tilly, Leila and Bradley, on the other hand, for some unknown reason, decided between them not to run away. Instead they followed Sybil Heliot into her house.

Sitting down together at the large table in the centre of the room, they held their noses at the pungent smell wafting from the cauldron. They glanced uneasily around them. It was Tilly who spoke first.

Gathering all the courage she could muster, she asked, "You're a real witch, then?"

Leila and Bradley gawped at her, not believing Tilly had just called Sybil Heliot a witch to her face. What would become of them now?

Without uttering a single word, Sybil Heliot moved over to the black pot. Picking up a large spoon, she began to stir the steaming, bubbling mixture inside it while the children watched on in alarm. They had read fairy tales where the witch put children into a cauldron like that. Was that what Sybil Heliot had in mind for them?

Finally, finishing her stirring, Sybil Heliot twisted round.

"Yes, I am a real witch." The children shivered. "However, I haven't come here to cast spells or turn children like you into frogs… Let me start from the beginning. I come from a land beyond the mountains…"

"There aren't any mountains in Essex…" piped up Bradley.

"Oh, yes there are, young man," snapped Sybil Heliot. "There are mountains human folk like you can't see, because you are not looking close enough. I have lived there for hundreds of years and I would still be there now if it wasn't for my wicked sister, Hagatha."

As soon as Sybil Heliot mentioned her sister, the children became aware of the cats gathering closer around them. Seemingly, hearing Hagatha's name had upset them.

"It's alright my beautiful kittens. I won't let her hurt you anymore," soothed Sybil Heliot, stroking the head of the nearest cat, a large tabby.

Tilly hadn't witnessed Sybil Heliot speaking in such soft tones before. It was quite a surprise. Then a black cat, with the greenest eyes, suddenly sprang onto Tilly's lap and snuggled in towards her. Tilly reached down and stroked its head.

"My sister has always been my biggest foe," Sybil Heliot continued. "Even as small children, we fought battles using magic that went on for days, but I never truly believed she could be so wicked... Several months ago, she put a curse on me from our family book of spells. It can only be removed by the reversal spell…" Sybil Heliot actually wiped a small tear from her eye. "The curse means that I'm slowly losing my powers. Soon I will no longer have any powers at all. The thought of being a witch without any powers is just too awful for me to even think about."

She pulled out an enormous handkerchief from the pocket of her green dress. A loud trumpeting sound vibrated through the air as she wrapped the cloth around her nose and blew.

Placing the little black cat gently on the floor, Tilly rose to her feet and made her way around the table and stood next to the sobbing witch. Reaching out towards her, she touched her hand. Perhaps she wasn't so evil after all.

"Why can't you just use the reversal spell?" asked Tilly softly.

Sybil Heliot looked down at her with her green, bloodshot eyes.

"Because Hagatha tore the page out of the spell

book and hid it somewhere in Dingleby Hall. I've been searching for it for months. When Mrs Kendal died and I heard your family were coming to live in the Hall, I began to bring things home so I could search them properly." She lowered her eyes. "I didn't mean to steal them. I just haven't had time to check them all thoroughly yet before I returned them."

Sybil Heliot walked over to a door in the far wall and opened it. The children followed her and gasped at what they could see, for the room beyond was crammed full of furniture and ornaments stolen from the Hall.

"How did you get it all here?" asked Bradley.

"A few months ago, I could have just waved my wand, but not now… I had to hire that awful man Mr Spencer, because he was the only one I knew who had a cart to carry it all in. For payment, he took that noisy donkey away."

At last, this was the confirmation Tilly had been waiting for. Willow was definitely with Old Man

Spencer. She couldn't wait to reunite her with Sam. However, for the moment there was a more pressing problem to deal with.

She glanced at Leila, who nodded.

"I think Leila and I found the reversal spell, stuffed in an ornament."

Sybil Heliot's eyes grew larger.

"Where? Where is this ornament, Tilly Millpepper?"

"We found it in a ditch next to the woods. I think, after hearing what you just said about Old Man Spencer, it must have fallen off his cart. I've put it in a safe place in the Hall. I'll have to ride home and get it."

"That stupid, stupid man!" Sybil Heliot screamed. "I could have already had my powers back if it wasn't for him!" She waved her fists angrily in the air. "Yes, go swiftly, Tilly Millpepper. I haven't much longer, before my powers have gone forever."

✳ ✳ ✳

Tilly didn't like leaving her brother and best friend behind, but she had no choice. The ponies were still tied securely to the tree when she emerged from the darkness of the wood into bright sunlight. She looked around for Dexter, but there was no sign of the little dog. With no time for an explanation to Sam, she untied him and leapt into the saddle and headed off for home at a fast canter. She had decided not to tell Sam yet the good news about Willow. There was plenty of time for that. Anyway, she felt she had already let him down once, so she would have to be pretty sure Willow was still with Old Man Spencer before she told him.

Arriving at the Hall, she was pleased to find that no one was at home. For one thing she had no doubt her parents would have wanted to know what she was up to and Ann would definitely want to know why Leila wasn't with her. Finding the door key hidden beneath a terracotta flowerpot, she let herself in and ran up the stairs two at a time. There she was, in a shoebox right at the back of her walk-in wardrobe, the Victorian lady in her blue dress and white bonnet. Picking her up, Tilly clutched her tightly before slipping her into her backpack.

Back outside, Sam was waiting patiently. Mounting him quickly, Tilly turned his head back towards Briary Woods.

* * *

In the crooked wooden house, three people were waiting anxiously for Tilly's return. Bursting through the front door, Tilly's face looked quite red and flustered.

"Here it is," she cried breathlessly, retrieving the Victorian figurine from her backpack. "There's a stopper at the bottom and inside is a piece of paper, which I believe is the recipe for the spell." Still holding the ornament tightly, she added, "I have a few questions first, though, before I hand it over."

Sybil Heliot looked at Tilly impatiently. "OK, if you must."

"Where are Bella and Orion?"

Sybil Heliot's face cracked a smile. "Bella is the little black cat who was sitting on your lap earlier and Orion is the cat your brother is now stroking. Hagatha put a spell on them while we were fighting and I can't remove it with reduced powers. The minute they leave the woods, they turn from being the cats they were born to be, into a girl and a pony."

"Wow!" exclaimed Leila and Bradley together.

"That's it!" cried Tilly. "I knew she reminded me of someone. Jelly cleans her paws in the same way Bella cleaned the back of her hand at the horse show…"

"Well observed. It was particularly painful for me to see Bella as a child, because you see she is actually my familiar. Do you know what a witch's familiar is, children?"

"Yes," replied Tilly, "I remember reading it in a

story. It's like your assistant."

"Well done, Tilly Millpepper. Bella *is* my assistant." She reached down and stroked her little cat, who was busy winding herself around her legs. "Hagatha, on the other hand, has a keen-eyed hawk called Magnon. He's Hagatha's spy. If you ever see a hawk, beware, it could be Magnon on a scouting mission for Hagatha... Now can I have...?"

"I've just one more question," insisted Tilly eagerly, to Sybil Heliot's continued frustration. "A boy and his dog disappeared from the woods a few months ago. Do you know what happened to them?"

Sybil Heliot exhaled. "Yes, also Hagatha, I'm afraid." She bent down and picked up the big tabby. "Meet Yee Zhu. The little marmalade cat by the fire is his dog. Unfortunately for them, they came across my house when Hagatha was on one of her visits. She turned them into cats after I pleaded with her not to do anything worse."

The children stared at the two cats in disbelief.

"Can you turn them both back?" pleaded Leila.

"If my powers return, I will certainly try," replied Sybil Heliot.

Relieved to be finally taking the Victorian figurine from Tilly, Sybil Heliot pulled out the stopper. Immediately, her face lit up when she held the yellowing paper between her fingers.

"Yes, yes, this is it! Thank you, Tilly Millpepper. Thank you from the bottom of my heart. Now, children, you must leave me to concentrate. I have to work fast."

Walking back outside, the children found a fallen tree trunk to sit on. They sat in silence for a while thinking about Sybil Heliot and her sister and about witches in general. Bradley picked up a stick and began prodding the ground, moving the dead leaves around as he imagined stirring a big black cauldron.

Finally, Leila broke the silence.

"No one is going to believe us, are they?" she sighed.

Tilly smiled. "Well, I for one have believed in magic for a while…" She stopped herself from saying anything about Sam in front of her brother.

"Why don't we just run away now?" suggested Bradley.

"We could. I don't think Ms Heliot would stop us, but aren't you curious about what's going to happen next?" asked Tilly.

Tilly had hardly finished her sentence when a loud boom sounded from within the house, causing the chimney pot to tumble from the roof. The children looked on in astonishment as a bright light, filled with thousands of minute colourful stars, suddenly whooshed up through the hole where the chimney pot used to be. It continued on through the overhead canopy of trees, travelling swiftly upwards to the sky above. Then the door of the crooked house flew open and Sybil Heliot emerged dressed all in black. In her right hand she was holding a wand, and on her head sat the black, pointy hat.

She took a deep breath. "I have my powers back! I can go home!" she howled, as she glided towards the children.

"I'm happy for you," said Tilly, "but what about Yee Zhu and his dog?"

Sybil Heliot chortled, "You don't have to worry about them anymore. They are already home.

Now I'm going to head over the mountains. Goodbye children and thank you. Without your help I would have been condemned to live here forever."

With a swish of her wand, the area around the house was caught up in a whirlwind. It spun for several seconds and then, like magic, everything was gone – the crooked wooden house, the cats and Sybil Heliot.

The children stood staring in amazement at the space where the house had once stood, and then, turning away, they sprinted from the woods. If they had stayed a bit longer, they would have seen the disturbing sight of a large hawk circling overhead. Screeching loudly, Magnon eventually flew off over the trees. His mission was to report back to his mistress in a kingdom far, faraway. Inevitably, the news that her sister Sybil had her powers back would make Hagatha very angry, very angry indeed!

CHAPTER 18

Together Again

WHEN THE children reached Dingleby Hall they found everyone was buzzing with excitement, including Dexter, who thankfully had managed to find his way home. You see, Poppa had just discovered that someone had unloaded the furniture and ornaments stolen from the Hall into one of the outside buildings.

"It's a miracle!" exclaimed Grammy and Poppa together.

"Where are we going to put it all?" asked Dad, scratching his head.

"The big question is where has it all come from," cried Mum.

The children stood and smiled. They knew that Sybil Heliot had simply waved her magic wand.

"Mum, Dad," began Bradley finally, "we know where it all came from and how it got here."

The grown-ups gawped at him in amazement.

Tilly stepped forward. "The thing is, Mum," she beamed, "Grammy and I were right. Sybil Heliot *is* a witch…"

"I've even got a picture of her crooked wooden house on my phone," added Bradley, proudly showing everyone the photos.

The grown-ups stood listening in silence to the children's story, adding gasps in the appropriate places. Then it was hugs all round. Whether they truly believed the children's story of witches and magic spells was unclear, but the children were safe and unharmed and, in the end, that was all that mattered.

The other extraordinary news was the safe return of Yee Zhu and his dog. They had both appeared out of nowhere on the doorstep of his parent's house. Apparently, Yee Zhu couldn't recall where they had been or how they had got home, but home he and his dog were, as healthy as when they had disappeared. So, everyone was overjoyed with that outcome, especially his parents, who vowed never to let their son out of their sight again.

✳ ✳ ✳

It was a week later. Leila and Tilly were in the tack room cleaning their saddles ready for the Pony Club ride the following morning. This was going to be Leila's last outing on Star. She and her mum would soon be heading home.

"The time's gone too quickly," sighed Leila.

"I hope you'll come again next school holiday. I can't guarantee such an exciting adventure, though," grinned Tilly.

"Try and stop me. It's been amazing. Who would believe we would meet a real witch and that you could talk to a horse! I don't know how you've not told Sam the news about Willow, by the way."

"Like I said, I was wrong before. Old Man Spencer is a bit of a rogue. He could have sold Willow on for all we know. Anyway, hopefully we'll find out tomorrow."

✶ ✶ ✶

It was a beautiful sunny morning when fifteen members of the Little Abbot Pony Club assembled in the yard of Jo's riding school. Following a full inspection, Jo led the way out on her huge bay hunter mare. Keeping to bridleways as much as they could, it took them over two hours to cover the five miles that eventually led them to the coast and the sea.

After riding along the beach, especially allocated for dogs and horses, they dismounted and took care of their ponies first before starting their picnics. Sitting on the warm sand with their backs against large boulders, they settled down to devour their food.

Finally, getting to her feet, Tilly walked over to

where Jo was sitting.

"Are we anywhere near where Old Man Spencer gives donkey rides?" asked Tilly.

Jo shaded her eyes from the sun and looked up.

"It's not far away. Edie told me you think Mr Spencer has Willow?"

"Yes, I think he does. Do you mind if Leila and I go and look for him?"

Jo glanced at her watch. "You've got about half an hour before we have to set off for home. So, if you're going, you'd better go now."

Saddling up their ponies again, Tilly and Leila headed off in search of Old Man Spencer. Jo was right – he wasn't far away.

Rounding a bend, they brought their ponies to a halt, whereupon Tilly leaned forward and stroked Sam's neck.

"Look Sam, there's a man giving donkey rides. Shall we take a closer look?"

There were only two donkeys this time, tied to the long rope. All the others were busy trotting back and forth with youngsters on their backs. As they drew nearer, Sam threw his head up and down.

"It's him, the man who took Willow away!" He started to trot quickly over the sand, leaving deep hoof prints as he went. "Is she here? Is Willow here?" he snorted.

"I'm not sure, Sam. You're the only one who would recognise her," replied Tilly.

Pulling their ponies to a halt, the girls dismounted. Together, they scrutinised the donkeys as they passed by. Then all of a sudden Sam let out an enormous whinny.

"Willow!" he called. "Willow, it's me Sam!"

A little donkey, with a thin white blaze on her nose, released an ear-splitting 'hee haw' and came trotting over. At the same time, the young boy bouncing on her back began to yell for his mother.

Hearing the commotion, Old Man Spencer marched towards them. His face was like thunder, while his large money belt jangled as he put one foot purposely in front of the other.

"Get those bloomin' horses out of here! They're upsettin' my donkeys!" he bellowed.

The screaming child's mother instantly appeared on the scene and pulled her offspring out of the donkey's saddle and out of harm's way.

Tilly and Leila stood motionless beside their ponies.

"Mr Spencer, remember me?" began Tilly. "I've come to take back the donkey from Dingleby Hall."

"What you talkin' about?"

"I think you know, Mr Spencer. This little donkey is Willow. Sybil Heliot gave her to you in exchange for the things you helped her steal from the Hall."

Immediately the colour drained from Old Man Spencer's haggard face. He glanced around him, afraid someone else might have heard Tilly calling him a thief.

"Take her! She's too much bloomin' trouble anyway. Take her now and let that be the bloomin' end of it," he growled, before stomping away.

✳ ✳ ✳

It was with much sadness that Leila left Star at the stables after returning from their ride. Stroking the pony's nose, she held out a handful of oats. Star threw her head up and down before munching on them gratefully. Then Leila led Willow back to Dingleby Hall, while Tilly rode on Sam. The two friends wondered how they were going to explain to Tilly's parents about Willow, but were sure under the circumstances they would understand. Releasing the pony and donkey into the paddock, they watched with delight as the pair nuzzled each other.

"Sam looks perfectly happy at last," smiled Leila.

"He does, doesn't he?" replied Tilly, leaning over the fence. "It's all come right in the end, hasn't it? Yee Zhu and his dog are back home. Great Aunt Phoebe's things are back in the Hall where they belong, and Sybil Heliot is a fully-fledged witch again and has disappeared out of our lives."

"Are you going to go back to that antique shop to show your mum the painting?" asked Leila.

"Yes, Mum said she would definitely have a look now," said Tilly. "I bet Uncle Leo has never had an adventure like we've had. I can't wait to tell him when he next visits."

* * *

The following afternoon, Tilly and her family stood on the platform at Millington Railway Station and waved goodbye to Leila and her mum, Ann. It was hard to say goodbye, but Ann promised they would both be back for half term.

The minute she reached home, Tilly raced up to the paddock and found Sam and Willow were busy munching grass together. She called Sam's name. He raised his head and trotted over to her.

"I'm so glad we managed to find Willow, Sam," she said, as she threw her arms around his neck.

Sam looked at her and snorted, but no words came from his lips. Tears rose in Tilly's eyes.

"Sam, talk to me, please?"

Still Sam said nothing. Tilly understood only too well what had happened. She hugged him tightly, then finally released him so he could go back to join Willow.

* * *

Getting ready for bed, Tilly removed the Wishing Stone from the back of her chest of drawers and gazed down at it. It really was a special wishing stone. It had made it possible for her to talk to Sam when he needed help, but now there was no need because he had Willow back in his life. Tilly was happy that Sam was happy, but sad that she couldn't speak to her pony friend anymore. Looking closer at the tiger, she couldn't be a hundred percent sure, but it seemed the tiger's paws were not quite as enormous as they were before. Placing the smooth, yellow stone back in the drawer, she realised she would have to be very careful about what she wished for in future.

Climbing into bed, Tilly pulled the covers up to her chin. It was then a furry face appeared. Jellicle felt it was way past her bedtime and snuggled down in the warm dip beside her.

"We might not be able to talk to each other, Jelly, but you always seem able to let me know what you want, don't you?" she smiled. Reaching out, she tenderly stroked the little cat's head. "Goodnight Jelly, sleep well."

The End

… but more is coming soon!

This is the first book in the Tilly Millpepper series. Look out for Tilly's next magical adventure in *Tilly Millpepper and the Enchanted Book*.

ACKNOWLEDGEMENTS

The old saying 'better late than never' couldn't be truer in my case, for I have finally fulfilled the dream I had as a young girl, sixty years ago; I have started writing a book series for children.

There are several people I would like to thank, first and foremost my daughter Claire, who encouraged me from the start by saying that I could do this. Thank you, Claire. Thank you also to my other daughter Sarah for her constant support.

Thanks also go to Nina for her wonderful illustrations, and to all at Cavalcade Books for their advice and patience in helping me bring *Tilly Millpepper and the Wishing Stone* to print.

CPSIA information can be obtained
at www.ICGtesting.com
Printed in the USA
LVHW091103020719
622836LV00007B/308/P

9 781999 621360